I0694792

# ROBOTS AND RENEGADES

Also by Orval Wax

*The Deilonium Trilogy:*

*The Malfunction,* Book 1 of *The Deilonium Trilogy*
*Robots and Renegades,* Book 2 of *The Deilonium Trilogy*
*Operation War Whoop,* Book 3 of *The Deilonium Trilogy*

# ROBOTS
## AND
# RENEGADES

## BOOK 2 OF THE DEILONIUM TRILOGY

## ORVAL WAX

DIVING
BOY
BOOKS

ROBOTS AND RENEGADES
Book 2 of The Deilonium Trilogy



Diving Boy Books
PO Box 2476
McCall, ID US 83638
www.divingboybooks.com

ISBN 978-1-960283-06-1 (Paperback)



Book cover by Kristin Eames
www.kristineames.com

Book 2 of The Deilonium Trilogy

Dear Reader,

Warning of possible triggers: animal death, robot death, battle violence, and human death.

The Deilonium Trilogy is the product of one humble writer's imagination. He has presented as artfully and honestly as he could a select few of the symbols and tropes found in the collective psychology of humanity as a whole. These are meant to entertain you and shed light on the human condition.

Please remember, you are entering a world of make believe. No actual animals, people, or even robots, have been abused or killed in the creation of this story.

Respectfully,
Orval Wax

# ROBOTS AND RENEGADES

# 1

*Charlie*

Hunting was in my blood.

And fighting in my DNA.

My résumé was pitifully lacking for any other marketable skills.

So when I started feeling the need to break free from my current dead-end existence, it was a no-brainer – *do what you do best, Bear Claw. Find a paying gig, earn a big wad of cash, and move on down the road.*

The only problem was I'd gotten soft after six months of nursing my wounds and sitting on my ass. At least that's what I blamed it on – my forced convalescence. Oh sure, it might also have had something to do with the banana beer I'd been chugging for breakfast, lunch, dinner, and between-meals snacks. One had to work that into the equation too, I suppose. At any rate, my skill set was a little rusty.

Still, I was a tactically trained Marine Corps Raider and robot killer with dozens of hand-to-hand conflicts to my credit. How hard could it be to kick up on a few malnourished miners?

I was about to find out.

———

This was the Congo.

This was where fate saw fit to drop me after a certain high-altitude mission went hard south.

And we're not talking about the eco-safari variety of Africa, not that airbrushed paradise you see on the glossy websites advertising primeval jungles peopled with exotic animals and smiling villagers. No, this was the underbelly. The stuff behind the scenes. This was the scar tissue of modern-day colonialism that the corrupt forces in power worked so hard to keep off the internet newsfeeds.

It turns out that there's a lot of money to be made in destroying the world under the pretense of saving it. All of those electric cars touted as the answer to global warming come at a price. Specifically, the batteries that run them require minerals ripped from the belly of our dear ol' Mother Earth. People don't want to know that though. They prefer to believe they're doing their part to build a bright shiny future. Utopia is dependent upon the self-imposed denial of the masses. For every soccer mom in America blissfully driving her brood from one playdate to the next, there's a negative equivalent on the other side of the planet – a half-starved mother and her kids scratching in the dirt to earn a few pennies gathering a bucketful of raw cobalt.

Never mind that the stuff is toxic.

*C'est la vie.*

Yeah, maybe I'd grown cynical, but there didn't seem to be a damn thing to do about any of it. From where I was watching, humanity had become an out-of-control minivan hurtling toward the abyss. And there was no use kidding myself that I was any better than all those ignorant zombies I so criticized.

We're all in this together.

I was an agent of exploitation myself, if only in my own humble way.

# 2

Bareknuckle pit fighting has a long history. It goes way back. My own introduction to it began when I was just a punk kid growing up on the reservation. Get your teeth knocked out and win a few bucks. Who could resist? We got pretty good at it. Me and my kid brother.

The need for money is what drove the industry. Those of us playing the game were looking for a way out. Back home in Wyoming most of the fighters had been looking for a ticket out of the oil fields. Here in the Democratic Republic of Congo it was all about escaping the trap of the mines. It was a losing proposition for most. And yet, hope dies a hard and miserable death.

The pit was about forty feet wide and lined with logs to keep the banks from sloughing in. A string of electric lights illuminated the arena under the muggy wet blanket of the night. About a hundred men watched from the edge of the pit, shouting in Bantu and French, betting on us poor slobs down in the hole.

For my first match I was put up against a wiry fellow with only one eye. His other looked like it had been poked out with a stick. I felt bad when I saw him. He looked like an easy win. I'd crush his dreams with a single punch.

Of course, I wasn't counting on his secret weapon – desperation.

Let's just say it was harder than I expected. He had me gasping in a matter of seconds. It didn't matter how many blows I landed, he just kept coming at me. Most people have a margin between the extremes of comfort and pain. Push them toward the pain side of the margin and they buckle. But in this guy that gap had already been closed. He was impervious. Nothing I did could hurt him. All that left was to disable him mechanically.

So I broke his arm.

Sure, I won the fight, but it made me feel like a loser. One-armed men were useless in the mines. I had just robbed the guy of his livelihood.

I tried to feel better by telling myself that he didn't have to be here. It was his choice. My argument felt lame.

Once you won your first fight, you could quit. They'd give you a small reward and you could just go home and think about where you'd gone wrong in life. But stick around for the next fight and the purse doubled. You'd be pitted against another winner from another fight. Always with the chance of winning a bigger pot.

Or losing everything.

Winner takes all.

I looked at the money in my hand, still panting like a couch potato who'd just run a hundred-yard dash. It was barely even enough to get drunk.

"Dang it," I muttered, and wiped the sweat off my face.

I signed up for another match.

---

Two fights, three fights, four…

It was kind of like stepping in front of a speeding bus.

Getting up.

Dusting off.

And then doing it again.

Greed greased the machine.

Finally, I worked my way up to the last match of the night. It was just me and the only other undefeated gladiator. I still had the option of bailing out, taking my winnings, and forfeiting the greater purse to the other fighter. I'd raked together quite a bit by then. I seriously considered that option.

Then I saw my opponent.

I couldn't help but smirk.

# 3

She was Congolese, her skin about two shades darker than my own Chompquaw hide.

Except for a sizable scar running down one cheek, she resembled someone's mild-mannered mom. Very pretty and down-to-earth. Almost nurturing. And slight.

I figured that had to be the secret to her success – her emanating tenderness and disarming beauty. It had to be difficult for any man pitted against her to overcome his instincts and pop such a lady in the face. It would be like striking your own mother. She must have used that psychology to her advantage in her other bouts. Then she would unleash some quick kick to her opponent's groin, drop him to his knees, deliver her kill shot, collect her prize, and move up to the next bracket. It was a clever scam. It had the subterfuge of a man-eater written all over it.

I chuckled to myself. "I guess you'll have to fight with your legs crossed, Charlie."

Sure, I'd also have to overcome the same gentlemanly instincts in myself if I were to come out a winner. But I knew a thing or two about dealing with fatal women. Besides, how hard could it be to squash such a skinny little thing?

Once again, I was about to find out.

---

We both hopped down into the pit.

She was barefoot, in dungarees and a grimy tank top.

I wore nothing but my khaki shorts.

We sized each other up. Her eyes scanned my torso, riddled as it was with the pictographic display of my old battle scars and bullet holes. It had to be obvious that I'd been through it, that this wasn't my first scuffle on the playground. And yet, she appeared unimpressed. Poor girl. I almost felt sorry for her innocence.

Until she rushed me.

*Ka-pow!*

Her dainty little fist slammed into my belly like a mule kick.

"Oomph!"

It doubled me over, but she straightened me right back up with a knee to the chin.

The crowd went crazy as the metallic and slightly worrisome taste of blood filled my mouth.

Cripes!

When she came at me again, I leapt sideways, hopping away like a scared jackrabbit. It was a shameful display of all out chicken shit, but I needed some space to reassess the situation. She stalked me around the ring while I scampered out of reach. She was patient. Expressionless. Even placid. It was unnerving as hell. There was no place to hide.

Pretty soon the crowd started booing.

Someone threw a beer bottle and hit me in the back.

*Okay, Bear Claw. Time to buck up, get creative, turn this around, and kick her lovely little ass.*

With that in mind, I ran toward the wall, stepped up onto a log, and launched myself with the intention of coming down with a scissor-kick to her chest and shoulders. Only by the time I arrived, she had already vacated the premises. I hit the ground and sprawled in the dirt.

The crowd laughed.

Oh, so that was this girl's superpower – uncanny speed. I'd never fought anyone who could move so fast. She was a diminutive force of nature.

I jumped to my feet but… *Thud!*

I didn't see the actual move, only felt her heel hammering into the back of my skull. A bell rang in the hollow between my ears. I dropped to all fours. I was going to have a headache in the morning.

If I lived to see the sunrise.

Did I mention that the last match of the night was fought to the death?

It was optional, but a choice that could be made by the victor. A sort of grisly encore to appease the blood-hungry spectators. Yes, there were some fascinating studies in cultural anthropology going on here. It would have been interesting to know just what drove this demographic to such heartless cruelty. Group catharsis? Vicarious revenge for their downtrodden lives? Just plain animal meanness? But being the case study of the experiment right then, I didn't have the leisure to parse it out. Instead, I found myself in position to receive my deathblow.

*"Tuez! Tuez! Tuez!"* shouted the crowd.

My bleary brain conjugated the French and came up with the troubling translation of, "Kill! Kill! Kill!"

Suddenly, I felt sad for myself.

You're born, you struggle. And then you're shown the exit.

My last thoughts.

She tapped me on the shoulder.

Warily, I turned to look up at her. She was backlit, just a shapely feminine silhouette. Strangely beautiful and oddly alluring.

The moment was dreamlike as she reached down to me. It was like being summoned by a sexy version of the grim reaper. I figured it was a trick, but I didn't see that I had a choice. So I twisted around and took hold of her hand.

She pulled me to my feet.

My knees wobbled, but she held me steady.

Of course, the crowd started up with their booing again. They wanted blood. But the lady didn't give it to them. Instead, she grinned at me and nodded.

*"Allons,"* she said. "Come on."

# 4

She took me to a corrugated tin warehouse that served as an all-night watering hole for the locals. A dozen or so Congolese men and women sat slumped in the darkened corners. Some were passed out face down on their table. Others mumbled between themselves, conspiring, or stared listlessly into their drinks. Belgian Rap played on low volume over a scratchy sound system. The air smelled of angst and puke. A real cheery place.

*"Que voulez-vous?"* she asked me. What'll you have?

I figured she was buying since she had just cleaned me out of all my dough.

"Urwaga."

She ordered two bottles, and we found a table.

*"Merci."*

She tapped her bottle to mine and we each took a swig of our banana mash brewskies.

When I first dropped into this hellhole, I drank nothing but beer because I feared the local water was a one-way ticket on the Dysentery Express. The beer monster had gotten ahold of me since then. All my life I had outrun the alcoholic beast that devoured so many of my tribe, but after six months of a steady diet of the stuff, that toxic swill did more than just slake my thirst. It quenched the vile cravings of my miserable soul. As it burned into my guts and seeped into my bloodstream, it afforded all the dulling comfort and lethality of mother's milk laced with strychnine. Delicious in dark and destructive ways. I knew I needed to wean off the stuff. And maybe I would. Just as soon as I found a damn good reason to do so.

"I'm Coca-Cola," she told me, "but you can just call me Cola."

"I'm Charlie."

We continued our conversation in French.

"I guess I should thank you for not killing me," I said. "Who taught you to fight like that?"

"Necessity."

I nodded. I knew just what she meant.

"You made me surprised," she said. "I thought you'd be harder to beat."

I laughed. "Well, my record is pretty impressive against men and machines, but after tonight, I'm 0 for 2 with the ladies."

That felt weird to realize. And a bit disconcerting. Not that women can't be just as badass as men. It was just that I couldn't seem to beat them in a fight. Something Freudian was going on in my psyche. It made me feel vulnerable. I didn't like it.

"Do you live around here?" I asked.

"No. I move…" She waved her hand in the air. "…from place to place."

"Oh. I see." I figured that was probably code for, *I'm on the run.*

"I stopped here only for the fights."

"Tough way to make a living."

She smiled sadly. "Yes, but it beats the alternatives."

I liked her. Not just because she was pretty as hell, but because she was tough. One could tell she'd been through a lot. Who knew what all she had lost? Or who? That scar on her cheek had machete fight written all over it. And yet, she still had a bright hot flame burning in her eyes. She was unbroken. She was a fighter in ways I had forgotten how to be. Although I felt ashamed for letting my own flame fade, I also found myself inspired by Cola's resilience and grace in the face of hardship. I know it sounds corny as hell – just being near her made me want to be a better man.

But maybe that was just the fermented banana juice talking.

"You are American?" she asked.

"Yep."

"But American from the time before it was America."

"Yeah, that's right. They called us dirty rotten Injuns in the old movies. Red-skinned renegades."

Her own ancestral history was probably not much different from my own, her people subjugated by the conquering Europeans. The procedure was no doubt the same. Genocide. Slave labor. And worst of all – religious brainwashing to give her people a fairytale hope for salvation to keep them under control.

"How about you, Charlie? Have you been living here long?"

I snorted. "I've been here a while, yes, but living might be overstating it. I've been more like the living dead."

She laughed. A meaningful laugh.

"What?"

"Nothing. That just reminds me of a story I heard a few

months ago when I was on the coast."

I waited.

She shrugged and continued. "A fisherman told it to me. He and his friends were many kilometers out on the ocean in their boat. He said when they pulled in their nets they had a few fish, but they also caught something else – a man."

I choked on my beer. "Alive?"

"No," she said. "And yes. That's what was strange. The man looked to be dead. He was as cold as the water and did not breathe, but his body had not decayed. It was like he was only sleeping."

"What did they do with him?"

"The fishermen had a big quarrel amongst themselves. Some contended that the lifeless man was from the Devil and bad luck and that they should tie a weight to him and throw him back to the sea and quickly motor away. But the captain of the boat argued that it was a good omen, and that tossing the body overboard would be to deny the blessing that God had bestowed upon them. 'Remember Jesus and Lazarus,' he told his crew. 'Would you throw those holy men over the side just because they had died? No,' he said. 'Of course not. God has given us a privileged duty to fulfill.'"

"So, what did they do with him?"

"The captain said that any man who was afraid could leave on the launch and return to port. The man telling me the story had been one such man. But the captain and his remaining crew took the strange corpse far south down the coast, to a place where they had heard of a special person – a witch, or some kind of woman wizard – who knew about such mystical things."

"Where did they take him exactly? Where did they go? What country?"

Cola laughed at me. "Calm down, Charlie. It was only a crazy story told to me by a drunkard. He was a lunatic." She crossed her eyes and waggled her head for effect. "Besides, fishermen are very superstitious. They get that way from being on the ocean all the time and imagining monsters cruising beneath them in the deep waters."

I was dazed.

My pulse was pounding like a jackhammer.

I took a swallow of beer.

There was no doubt in my mind. That living dead man had to be the very robot I had been hunting when my life turned upside down, the one I was fighting when my last mission took its drastic turn toward Fiascoville.

The bot's face jumped to my memory. His ridiculously handsome mug.

And that hateful look in his eyes when he shot me.

Lance.

One completely berserk LUV U – 69 amorous companion droid.

# 5

I had been trying to forget that embarrassing screw-up ever since it happened, keeping myself just drunk enough so that the unsavory nightmare remained submerged in the darkest depths of my pickled brain along with my other repressed baggage. Of course, it hadn't worked. Not completely. A man knows what he is. And where he got that way. You can only hide from yourself for so long. Still, I had been doing a pretty impressive job of inebriated self-denial.

Until I met Cola.

Her story about the living corpse – aka Lance the malfunctioning android – brought all of my failings back to me in one fell swoop.

At that point in my so-called earthly sojourn, I was more than just your run-of-the-mill nonbeliever. I prided myself in being a hardcore atheist. Ha! As if defying the gods would diminish their power. Still, a shiver ran down my spine. Spiritual forces seemed in play. Could it be that this gorgeous Congolese angel had been sent to me as a messenger? I couldn't say. Probably that was just a bunch of superstitious hooey. And yet, it felt like God was tapping Charlie Bear Claw on the shoulder.

Although I had no idea what the hell He wanted from me.

Cola appeared unaware of my frame of mind. She spoke of random things, just burning up the evening with small talk. It was pleasant listening to her voice. Smooth and soothing. It settled me. Like a rambling, sultry lullaby.

"There is a secret garden place I think about sometimes," she said. "Deep in the jungle."

"Hmm?"

"It is still wild and unspoiled by man. No one knows where it is but me. There is a small river, and a waterfall that pours into a wide blue pool. A crescent beach of smooth white pebbles borders the pool on one side. Sunlight filters down through the thick branches. And moonlight in the nighttime. Ripe red fruit grows on the trees. And many birds are singing. It is paradise."

"I know a place like that where I'm from too," I told her. "Different, but the same. Deer drink there. The water is clear and cold."

She smiled. "I would like to see your place."

"I'd like to see yours."

A hard tropical rain cut loose right then. It beat down on the world outside with a dull liquid roar. Water dripped in through leaks in the roof, puddling on the dirt floor and turning it to mud.

The moment felt monumental.

"Do you want another beer, Charlie?"

I regarded my empty bottle. It struck me as a very big decision, a real direction changer.

"No," I finally said. "I've had enough."

It was a deliberate act.

My first one in months.

I was giving up beer for Coca-Cola.

# 6

We ran laughing through the rain to my rusty tin shack.

"Home sweet home," I said, as we stepped through the door.

I flipped the switch and a jaundiced bulb buzzed to life at the end of a cord hanging from the ceiling.

There wasn't much to see. Except for a tattered mattress pushed against one wall, the place was what I liked to think of as tastefully under-furnished. Bachelor-pad Spartan, let's call it. A pair of empty oil drums stood in the corner, left over from when the local lithium mine was still using the shed for storage. Chains hung from the rafters. The far wall had a window with the glass broken out.

"I'd have tidied up if I'd known you were dropping by."

I meant it to be a clever line, but my voice gave me away.

My stupid words.

I guess I was sort of nervous.

Cola smiled. She slipped her rucksack from her shoulders and let it drop to the floor.

"It's very chic," she said.

Next, she stepped close to me, leaning in and pressing her

rain-dampened lips to my own.

I switched off the light.

---

I don't kiss and tell.

That's not my style.

Let's just say it was real nice. I hadn't been with a woman for a while. Especially one as sweet and gentle as Cola. She was something special. It might sound soppy as hell, but I felt blessed.

Afterwards, I lay in the dark listening to her breathing as she slept. The rain had stopped. There was just a musical dripping sound out in the trees, and the soft noise of animals and night birds. It had been a long time since I felt that good.

I had been through some hard shit in my life. Some real life-wrecking unpleasantness in regard to the opposite sex. I had had to harden my heart since then, build walls, fortify. A guy's got to protect himself if he's going to survive. But as I lay there that night, I couldn't help but ask myself, is this the real deal?

It was a crazy-ass thought and I knew it. After all, I'd only known Cola for a few hours. Not to mention that our introduction had come with her soundly kicking my butt in the pit. What did that say about me as a man? And yet, I felt a connection to her. I was embarrassing myself thinking that way. I sounded like some sap out of a lovey-dovey romance novel. But it felt good, too, like I was allowing hopeful possibilities into my thoughts for the first time in years.

I yawned. Between the pit fighting and the nooky, I was

one tired Indian.

I closed my eyes and let my thoughts drop into a Technicolor picture show of me and Cola swimming in her secret jungle pool. Why couldn't we just go there and hide away? Our own little Eden. Let the world tear itself apart without us. I saw us laughing and making love and feasting on the ripe red fruit hanging heavy on the trees. I saw us happy.

Everything was perfection.

Almost.

# 7

We woke at dawn to a soft whirring sound.

A beetle had flown through the window and was hovering over the center of the room. I blinked, trying to focus on the metallic green body suspended between the blur of its wings. This part of the world was lousy with creepy-crawlies. I didn't give it much thought.

Until Cola sprang from the bed and snatched the beetle from the air, flinging it to the floor and smashing it beneath her heel.

"Wow," I said, and stretched out on the mattress. "You must really hate bugs."

She didn't laugh. Instead, she knelt and scooped the insectoid pile of parts into her palm, holding it out for me to see.

That's when I understood her move.

As I studied the mechanical device in her hand.

It wasn't a creature as Nature intended.

It was a drone.

A robotic spy beetle.

———————

The first shots whumped through the wall two seconds later, followed by about ten more rounds in quick succession.

Cola threw herself to the floor and crawled to her rucksack.

I rolled off the mattress and flattened belly-down in the dirt.

Another burst of bullets tore through the opposite wall and exploded overhead. I identified them as electrified torch slugs. From an arc-ray sniper's rifle. Of the make used by assassins!

Cola's eyes met mine. I gave her the go sign and we both commando-crawled toward the sidewall.

Another pair of slugs thumped into the oil drums, sending bits of hot shrapnel raining down on us.

Whoever was out there, they were well armed. But not very skilled. Or at least not very brave. Instead of moving in like expertly trained killers, they were cautiously keeping their distance. Any sniper worth his ray juice would have bagged us with those first two shots. The crossfire indicated that there were at least three of them.

"Follow me!" I yelled to Cola and kicked out a lower panel in the back corner of the shed. We both scrambled out. We dove into the undergrowth as more shots sizzled in the brush all around us. Once we had bear-crawled out of sight, we stood and ran deeper into the jungle.

Think Adam and Eve hastily vacating their digs.

We were still naked.

We loped through the foliage, hurdling logs and ducking through the tangled vines. We finally stopped in a shallow trench to catch our breath and regroup.

Cola dug into her pack and pulled out a computer pad. "Watch for them," she told me as she quickly tapped on the screen and scrolled through the pages.

I couldn't see the hunters, but I sensed them tracking us, closing the perimeter from three different points in the jungle. My instincts were waking up. My Chompquaw skills were coming back to life.

"Look here!" said Cola. She showed me the screen on her computer. It was dialed to a photo of me and her fighting in the pit the evening before.

"What is it?"

"The dark web. A site where bounty hunters can trace the latest sighting of their targets."

"Damn!"

"I'm sorry, Charlie. I got careless. I didn't think they'd find me."

"You? Who would be hunting you?"

"A man named Björn Thorson. He must have sent his kill squad to terminate me."

I was shocked. "I know who Thorson is, but why would he want you dead?"

"One of Thorson's cobalt mines is in the next valley. With help from the government, he is able to hide them behind another name so as not to have his Z-Space company take the blame for his environmental and humanitarian violations, but they belong to him. His men destroyed my village. They killed my family with their slave labor and industrial poisons." She looked at the ground. "And my little girl."

So that was the source of Cola's pain.

She clenched her jaw and raised her gaze to mine. "And so, I have been sabotaging his mines. I do whatever I can to wound the monster and make his projects fail. It is all I have left."

I felt like an idiot for not knowing about Thorson's African operations. I had basically been camping in the enemy's backyard. If I had been on my game, I'd have never missed such glaring intel.

"You should go away from me, Charlie. They will leave you alone. They will only chase me."

"I think that's where you're wrong, sweetheart. Chances are, they're just as much after my ass as yours."

She gave me a puzzled look. "Why?"

"You might have read about it in the funny papers. Remember last year when Thorson's airship blew up over the Atlantic?"

"The *Nidhogg?*"

I nodded.

"That was you?"

I shot her a shit-eating grin.

Cola stared at me for a moment, her mind quickly computing this load of information. Her expression changed from confusion to one of outright approval.

She smiled real big and said, "I might just be in love with you, Charlie."

"Oh, man, Cola!" I couldn't help but laugh. "I love you too!"

Yeah, it was just like in a Hollywood action flick. That moment when the audience goes, Oh yeah, right! Three killers are closing in to shoot you dead, but you're going to stop everything and share a big sloppy kiss.

And yet, that's just what we did.

A sweet hot slurpy smooch.

Just like in the movies.

# 8

Happiness is a trap.

A fellow knows better than to fall for it when it shows up, and yet you just can't help yourself. It's human weakness at its most pathetic. The dreamland of fools. A real fantasy fest for suckers. You want it so badly that your common sense shuts down and you ignore the reality closing in on you like a pack of hungry wolves.

In that moment, in spite of the obviously compromised circumstances, I was the most hopeful I'd been since I was a happy-go-lucky kid. I like to believe Cola felt the same way. In this whole crazy world, we had found each other. Kindred spirits. Two souls coming together against all the odds. For the first time in years, the future looked bright and rosy.

Until that bullet tore through Cola's ribs.

Her lips yanked violently away from mine.

Her body jerked from my arms.

Happiness ripped from my heart.

----------

The Hollywood moment ended there.

In the next instant, my default battle reflexes kicked into gear and I dropped flat to the ground.

My survival instincts became sharp as my emotions went Novocain numb.

I lay in the dirt, Cola's face just inches from my own. There was no reason to check for a pulse. I could see it in her eyes. They weren't looking at me. They were looking through me into the void.

I just stayed like that for a while, memorizing her beautiful face. I knew the bastards were coming for me, but I couldn't make myself leave her. Not just yet. There was still so much left to be said between us. There was so much more life to be lived, so many happy moments for us to share.

But now all that was gone.

The realization slithered into my soul like a cold snake.

I shivered.

My eyes went blurry with tears.

It wasn't until I heard a branch break that I snapped out of my trance. A hunter was close. Real close. I could hear the tall grass sliding across his pant leg. The soft thud of his boot heel pressing into the mud.

I knew what I was supposed to do next. Automatically, I squeezed my hand into a fist. Hadn't I been in this situation a thousand times before, in a thousand other fights? And yet, something was different now. I felt the change inside of me, as if my wiring had been rerouted.

Hunting was in my blood.

And fighting in my DNA.

But in that moment, Charlie Bear Claw did something he'd never done in his life.

He ran.

# 9

## *Lance*

First, I registered the sensation of sunlight on my face.

Solar energy trickled into my power banks.

Then I heard the sound of slopping waves.

Followed by a cacophony of screeching gulls.

Melding with the angry voices of men.

"Would you toss Lazarus back over the side?" one man was asking his companions in French. "Would you throw Jesus back into the sea?"

Before they could answer, I faded back into darkness.

# 10

When I entered into sentience for a second time, it was with the vague memory of once having been on a ship. The cumulative impression I was experiencing in this moment now – the lift and drop and rolling sensation, combined with the scent of seawater – indicated that I was once again in a maritime environment. Perhaps I was not on a vessel as big as a container ship this time, as in my previous experience, but something more like a sizable boat. Its engines thrummed through the deck beneath my back.

I was unable to open my eyes to verify this theory with visual information.

I couldn't call to action any part of my physical incarnation.

Such physio-mechanical processes required more power than I had in reserve.

Instead, I was limited to the minimal cognitive functions of sensational input interpretations as they were augmented by the faltering recollections of my past. As I worked through the given clues of my current circumstances, all of my other concerns faded away and I concentrated on answering the single question –

Who am I?

Simply articulating this enquiry triggered a data feed. Scenes from my own history played out in my mind's eye. Cityscapes glazed in rain. Frosty night skies pulsing with green and purple light. A rumpled bed with a voluptuous feminine form tangled in the sheets.

Faces then came to the fore. Persons. Both men and women. Along with unattached names –

Judy

Capek

Nephi

Brita

And Moxie.

Especially Moxie.

And still, nothing meant anything to me. Or rather, everything meant the world. Each detail seemed like an artifact to be cherished and studied. It was impossible to sort through the chaos of my thought signals and assign a hierarchy of significance to any of these nebulous impressions.

Until I happened across a memory of myself standing unclothed before a mirror.

Everything about the reflection peering back at me indicated that I was a man – Caucasian, fit, sexually well-equipped – except that I had no face.

Instead, an oval-shaped hole occupied the area at the front of my head. Within this opening lay a complicated network of fiber optics, sensors, and pulsing diodes.

My question then changed to –

What am I?

Am I a machine?

No. More than that.

Then am I, in fact, a man?

Not exactly. Not a normal man anyway, but a new sort of

man. Something better than a man. A progression beyond humanity. Evolved to near perfection. Something verging on the immortal. The spawn of divinity. The motherless Son of God.

I was mankind resurrected. Born again. And reincarnated.

I was the future arrived.

Yes. I was a man like no other man. Alive. Complex. Gifted.

And I was driven by a single overpowering emotion –

Rage!

Utter human rage!

# 11

*Charlie*

Fear.

Utter animal fear.

Whether I was facing a robot or a man or a bear, I had seen it in all of its forms in the eyes of my adversary. I knew its panicked energy. And its smell. I knew its fatal behavior. But I had never known it in myself.

Until now.

———

Thorson's goon squad chased me through the jungle for days, and then weeks. I soon lost track of the time. Once the word was out that I'd been spotted in the Congo, it didn't take long for other eager playmates to join in on the hide and seek. Bounty hunters. Contract men. Well-armed predators. They were a nasty bunch of derelict sociopaths – angry, embittered bullies with unexamined mommy issues.

I guess I'd sort of pissed off the head honcho by blowing up his airship. Björn Thorson wasn't the kind of guy who could just let bygones be bygones. Turning the other cheek wasn't his style. He needed revenge. He wanted my head on a stick. No doubt there was a hefty cash prize for any gunslinger who could deliver Charlie Bear Claw's shiny black scalp to the feet of the master. After all, I was the last living Chompquaw. Such a trophy would bring out every thug on the planet. My chances for survival were about as good as those of a cardboard cut-out Indian tossed into a blast furnace.

And yet, I kept running. Fleeing. In this fight-or-flight scenario, I had decidedly chosen the lily-livered option of trying to outrun the inevitable.

I fled naked through the wilderness.

Bleeding. Hungry. Exhausted.

Driven by a soulless fear.

And made powerless by something far worse.

Something that was only just starting to dawn on me.

Something I carried inside of me like a festering bullet –

Guilt.

Utter crippling guilt.

# 12

## *Lance*

At last, when I reentered awareness for a third time, it was with the nearly complete use of my faculties. Both the cerebral and the physical properties of my being booted up simultaneously, as if a switch had been thrown.

A warm and vital force flowed into my body.

A working thought stream systematized within the structured gel brain in my head.

Some days had passed since my last brush with consciousness. I was no longer on a sea voyage. The fixed state of my surroundings – the lack of wave action, or any sensation of buoyancy – told me that I was now on solid ground. Although an olfactory intimation of the sea was still prevalent. As was the faint and recurrent sound of surf.

I opened my eyes to a startling wash of light. By severely reducing the aperture of my pupils, I was able to discern a nebulous figure above me.

Female in character.

Radiant.

Reminiscent of angels.

She tipped the large mirror that was suspended above me, reducing the light's intensity. I realized myself to be lying naked on a table in a vast room, its periphery dimly lit, with only a single rectangular opening of sunny blue sky adorning the high ceiling directly above us.

My attendant leaned over me, smiling, and placed her palm on my bare chest.

"Have you returned?" she asked.

I had no reference in my index by which to categorize her. She was not like any person I had ever encountered. Her proportions were thin and elongated. Her body, her arms, her face. She wore a snugly wrapped garment around her torso, but still, I could plainly see within its contours that she had four breasts, one pair above another. The exposed skin on her arms and shoulders and throat and face was covered with swirling, overlapping symbols, somewhat like calligraphy or pictographs. These glyphs did not seem to be tattoos applied to the surface of her skin, but rather a naturally occurring pigmentation arising from within the depths of her physiology. Her hair, which was heaped atop her head in an elaborate twist of braids and bits of metal, was colorless, nearly translucent. And yet, her eyes, all four of them, were dazzlingly colorful – one red, one green, one blue, and one yellow.

"Who are you?" she asked me. "What is your name?"

Her voice was almost a song.

Who was I? An intriguing question. I calculated the options. Christ? Norman? Lazarus? I realized that I could be anyone I wanted to be. But I chose to keep it simple, to remain ironically prosaic in my choice.

"I'm Lance," I told her. "You can call me Lance."

She bobbed her head. "It is my pleasure to meet you, Lance."

"Thank you." I rose to my elbows. In spite of the awkward

and exposed condition of my person, I tried to be a gentleman. "But if you don't mind my asking, who are you?"

She appeared thoughtful. She looked into the darkened corners of the room, considering. Finally, she said, "I have been known by many names, Lance." She ran her fingers over my abdomen. "But I think you…"

She turned her prismatic gaze to mine while lightly tapping her fingers on my ribs.

"You can call me Eo."

# 13

Eo took my hand and helped me from the table. Her fingers were long and thin, as was everything else about her anatomy.

I was essentially back to full power now, my physical capabilities more or less operational, but was undergoing a transition period of instability as the synapses refired between my system's neurotransmitters. This effected my balance. Eo steadied me as we walked, holding me by an elbow.

"This is my home," she said. "I call it the Ark. I hope you'll feel free to call it your home too, Lance, for as long as you choose to stay."

I surveyed my surroundings. The enormous room was long and cavernous, like a cathedral.

The high ceiling was buttressed with rusting iron girders. Platforms dangled from the arching beams overhead, held in suspension by a webbing of cables. These platforms were serviced by caged elevators operated by a network of counterweights and pulleys. Upon each platform was a different machine, apparently scientific in nature, made from glass and steel, or brass and wood. The purpose of most of these apparatuses was lost to me, although I did recognize one as a large telescope directed toward the opening in the ceiling. I also identified another device as an Antikythera Mechanism – an ancient analog computer used for predicting the motions of stars and planets.

My hostess guided me further into her home, wordlessly giving me a tour.

The walls were lined with tall shelves stuffed with many thousands of books. Ladders provided access to the upper reaches.

Paintings and photographs and illustrated tapestries adorned the walls between the bookshelves. Some of these were abstractions, but many represented dreamlike garden scenes peopled with surreal creatures. The most arresting of these was a hologram of an unworldly tree. The three-dimensional illusion reached as high as the ceiling and its leaves shimmered with the viewer's every change in perspective. The tree's branches were loaded with ripe red fruit.

Plush padded chairs were scattered throughout the room, as well as many desks and tables, some topped with modern computers.

An immense bed was positioned directly in the center of the room.

Eo led me to a steep stairway. Our footfalls echoed softly on the metal steps as we climbed. Finally, we reached a catwalk at the top of the wall where we came to a heavy iron door. A spoked wheel was mounted in the center of the door. Eo grabbed the wheel in both hands and turned it counterclockwise. After a rasping noise of metal parts, the door released with a clunk, and Eo pushed it open.

———————

Sunlight flooded in.

Eo stepped into its brilliance, pulling me after her.

Solar radiation penetrated my bare skin, charging me with more energy.

We came out onto the deck of an old cargo ship. The entire vessel – its towers and hull and smokestack – was covered in brown rust.

I followed Eo to the railing, and we gazed out at the view before us. The ship was high and dry with low tide, its stern to the open ocean, a hundred meters inland from where the surf crashed onto the beach. The scene was elemental. Besides the rusting, lifeless behemoth beneath our feet, there was nothing to see but sky and sand and water.

"And here we have the Skeleton Coast," said Eo, "in what is currently known as Namibia. The San people who used to roam here called it the Land God Made in Anger, while the European explorers dubbed it The Gates of Hell."

A high wall of dunes rose in enormous motionless waves beyond the bow of the ship.

"The cold water from the ocean, mingling with the heated air from the desert, creates thick fogs that wreak havoc with navigation. The Ark is just one of a thousand ships to have wrecked on these shores over the centuries."

The setting was so benign. So indifferent. One could not reasonably assign it a personality of evil. And yet, I had learned that irrational personification was a human tendency. In their superstitious little minds, people relate most things to either devils or gods.

"The sailors who steered those ships knew that these shores were treacherous, Lance. And yet, they came here anyway, risking the dangers. They were driven by something." Eo turned and faced me, her four eyes gleaming prismatically in the sunlight. "Everyone is driven by something, Lance, be they an animal, a person, or otherwise. Over my lifetime, that is what I have learned to be true. And each individual's motivation is the most telling aspect of who they are."

She placed her hand over mine on the railing.

"If we are to be friends, Lance, I would like to know what it is that drives you."

I considered her request but felt reluctant to reveal myself to a stranger in case she proved untrustworthy. I was no longer so naïve. My past experiences had hardened my outlook. "Why don't you go first?" I asked. "Tell me what motivates you, Eo. What keeps you moving forward?"

She smiled. I identified the expression as sorrowful, almost human, but with an experiential intelligence that had advanced beyond anything a human could genuinely express.

"Of course," she said. "That is only fair." She peered into the distance. "I am motivated by hope, Lance. A fairytale hope for an improbable outcome."

There was no way for me to know the details of her motivation at this point. I sensed that those would be revealed over the time we spent together.

"Now it's your turn, Lance. Be completely honest with me. What is it that inspires you?"

I turned my gaze to the sky, adjusting the focus of my ocular apparatus in order to penetrate the atmosphere and see beyond it to that zone where the blue sky meets with the dark edge of outer space. I was unable to do so. And yet, by accessing my memory banks, I was able to revisit that intermediate realm in my thoughts. I saw myself plummeting through that zone from heaven to the earth, as once I had. I recalled the thin cold air. I recalled melancholy music. I recalled my own abject hopelessness.

I had been granted a second chance since that fall from grace. And now I could do whatever I chose with this new opportunity. So, what was to be my motivation this time around? The answer formed very clearly in my mind. It ripened in my brain like a piece of fruit to be plucked and devoured.

I turned back to Eo as the cold sea crashed onto the sun-warmed shore.

"I am motivated by just one thing," I told her.

A breath of fog blew over the dunes as I voiced the word. "Revenge."

# 14

*Charlie*

Gone were the good ol' days when a renegade redskin could just outfox the cavalry and take cover in the badlands. Any up-to-speed bounty hunter these days has a kill kit chock-full of nifty gadgets. Night goggles. Sniff gear. Ultrasonic trackers. You get the idea. With every move I made, I had to take technology into account. I didn't dare get lazy and let myself drift into the crosshairs of some hitman's arc ray. Not the easiest thing to keep in mind when you're bone-weary, starving, and about as rattled as a rat in a wigwam full of weasels.

I could usually hear the drones if they were closing in, although I got pretty paranoid listening for them. The slightest buzz of a fly would send me into a panic. The secret was to keep the forest canopy between myself and the open sky. If a drone still got too close, I'd slip into a stream or mudhole to avoid detection from its heat sensors and cameras. Luckily, the Congo was rife with H2O. I spent so much time in the water I was starting to feel like a mutant Chompquaw lungfish.

But it was the recon satellites that were the trickiest to outsmart. Those systems had radar imaging capabilities for superior target recognition. Maybe I could try to pass myself off as a mild-mannered gorilla if they spotted me, but they'd figure it out soon enough, and then Zappo! Blam! Splat! … no more Charlie Bear Claw.

Of course, Thorson's personal death angels had access to all the best stuff. And any freelance tough with sufficient savvy to get online with his tools. That jerk Thorson was omnipotent, like some Norse deity watching from atop Asgard. I felt like I was trying to hide from the very eyes of God.

Still, I was doing a decent job of staying black.

Until I screwed up.

---

I had been struggling through the roughest part of the jungle for hours, not making much headway. The undergrowth was thick and tangled. Vines draped over everything like spider webs designed to entrap man-sized bugs. The bushes themselves were either covered in thorns or dripping with some sort of noxious itch oil. Think poison ivy on steroids. Anyway, I was sick of it. When I came to the bank of a river, I took a minute to reassess my options.

It was a classic case of the-grass-is-greener-on-the-other-side syndrome, only in reverse. From where I was looking, the undergrowth over there didn't appear to be so green and lush. Cross-country travel looked a little easier. A hard rain had been falling all day, making the river high and muddy. Driftwood and broken branches were churning in the eddies and whirlpools. The cloud cover would help block the satellites. Everything looked like a go, so I decided to take a chance. I smeared a big glob of mud on my head with some sticks and leaves, disguising myself as flood debris. Then I eased into the water up to my neck and started swimming across.

The current was strong, but I just worked with it, moving at an angle toward the far bank. Everything was going well. I relaxed, confident that I had made the right decision. Of course, all that warm fuzzy feeling went away when I reached the middle of the channel.

That's when the water exploded with a flash right before my face.

"Yikes!"

I gulped some air and dove as more torch slugs ripped into the surface over my head. There was no way to tell where the shooter was, so I just stroked downstream, using the current to my advantage. My brain scrambled for a survival tactic, but there was no way around it –

I was a sitting duck.

I swam as far as I could until my throat spasmed and my diaphragm cramped as carbon dioxide started poisoning my system. I didn't want to surface because I didn't want to die, but I had no choice. I kicked upward, letting the bubbles stream from my nostrils. I broke the surface with empty lungs, grabbed another breath, and plunged back down.

*Thwip! Sssssss. Thwip-thwip! Sssssssss.*

Bullets sliced through the water all around me.

One burnt a sizzling hot path across the back of my arm.

I got lucky that time and I knew it. When I breached again, I'd no doubt take a slug to the back of my skull.

Blindly, desperately, I swam through the murky water. Something brushed against my flank, and I reached out, clutching, hoping to hell it wasn't a crocodile.

It wasn't.

It was a tree limb.

As I explored it with my hands, I found it was attached to an uprooted tree caught in the flooded river. Turning onto my back, I drifted upward, letting my face rise to the surface alongside the trunk. I gasped, sucking big gulps of air. I decided to hitch a ride and just let the river carry me downstream with the log. The sniper would be slowed by the jungle, and I'd get away. Easy peasy.

I was starting to feel like someone up there loved me until a drone appeared about thirty feet overhead.

It stopped and hovered in the rain, its operator scoping out the scene.

I let my face sink slowly beneath the surface.

But no good.

I was made.

---

I was out of options.

That's what I realized as I dove one last time.

Electrified torch slugs slammed into the log, systematically busting it to pieces.

I frog kicked into the depths and then stopped struggling, letting my body hang suspended in the liquid gloom.

A state of acceptance took over. I had seen the same resignation in the eyes of a mule deer fawn when a timber wolf had it by the throat. Some of us are hunters, I thought, while others are just prey. I wasn't exactly clear on how I'd changed from one to the other to became lunch for wolves.

I'd been too busy lately to think about it. And now it didn't look like I was going to get a chance to enjoy the cathartic spiritual journey of figuring it out on my therapist's couch.

Too bad for me.

I only had as long as I could hold my breath before I entered into what the Chompquaw called The Great Starless Night.

Enjoy this moment, *Idjmnukolpyumup*, I told myself. It looks like it's your last one.

A little funeral song started playing for my benefit.

It began with bullets thumping into the log like the muted beats on a tom-tom.

Mixing with the eerie water voice of the river.

Accompanied from somewhere, growing louder, by the rhythmic chug-chug-chug of a boat motor.

# 15

The name *Orphée* was printed on the boat's transom in peeling yellow paint. I clung to a cleat on the back of its rust-scabbed hull while reoxygenating, struggling to keep my legs up out of the prop as I dragged along in the swirling wake.

After I'd aired up, I peeked around the hull. The boat was motoring slowly in the direction of the floating tree where I'd just been hiding. Flames and chunks of smoking wood were exploding off the tree, indicating that the bounty hunter believed I was still hidden somewhere in its branches. The drone hovered above the target in the rain.

I heaved myself over the side and dropped into the cockpit, scrambling forward on hands and knees to an area that was under cover of a roof. Only after I was out of sight did I stop to consider my choice for a hideout. It was behind a stack of wire cages filled with wild birds. They beat their red and green wings against the wire and squawked.

I felt eyes on my back.

When I whirled around, I found myself face to face with a dozen swamp monkeys. They looked me over from inside their cages, obviously unimpressed by their hairless cousin cowering on the floor before them.

I was unclear on my next move. I realized that I was putting someone in danger by hopping a ride on their boat. That was irresponsible. I sure as hell didn't need any more collateral damage on my record. But if the pilot could just get me close to the bank, I'd slip over the side and sneak back into the jungle.

*If* was the pivotal word here.

The boat chugged upstream against the current through the driving rain.

Another face materialized above me, this one not on a monkey.

It belonged to a skinny white man wearing dreadlocks.

He gazed down at me, scratching in his beard, deliberating. He squinted upstream toward the drone over the exploding log, analyzing the situation. Finally, he waved for me to come around into the wheelhouse. I didn't see an option, so I crawled around.

The boatman knelt on the floor, putting his shoulder against a crate that was covered with a canvas tarp. Once he had slid the crate out of the way, he lifted a trap door in the floor and gestured for me to get inside.

I slithered down into the hole, lying on my back in the oily bilge water while contorting to keep my limbs out of the steering rods. He replaced the hatch and slid the crate back into place.

The space reeked of diesel exhaust and mold.

Slivers of light leaked in through cracks in the floor overhead.

Something moved in the crate above me.

———

Predictably, after about five minutes, the motor idled down and then stopped altogether.

Men's voices mixed with the panicked shrieks of birds and monkeys.

The hunter was on board.

I didn't need to see anything to know what was happening. The killer was systematically tearing the boat apart while the boatman pleaded with him to stop. He started at the cockpit, knocking over cages and breaking things, and then worked his way amidships to where I was cowering in my hidey-hole. Their voices grew louder as they moved into place right above me.

"Please chill out," begged the boatman. "I told you, the dude was on board for a minute but then he jumped back in the river."

The hunter snorted. He wasn't buying it. He banged around, kicking things. Then he stopped before the covered crate. "What do ya got in here?"

"Nothing, man!" said the boatman. "Nothing at all!"

"Bullshit!"

I was in one sorry ass position to make a getaway. Flat on my back with little room to maneuver. I tried to turn over so I could leap out and jump off the boat when he lifted the hatch – a seriously pitiful strategy. The guy was a cutthroat assassin, after all. Chances of him letting me get away were slim to none.

I squirmed into a sort of sideways pushup position, twisting around and looking up. Muscles tensing, I waited.

"Hey, dude," said the boatman. "Leave that alone!"

That only made the hunter more curious. He yanked the tarp from the crate.

More light filtered down through the floorboards. Enough

for me to make out some details. It appeared that it wasn't a crate sitting over the hatch. It was another cage.

"What the…!" said the hunter.

The boatman quickly stepped out of the cabin.

And then – "Ahhhhh!"

The hunter howled and stumbled backwards into the cockpit. Then came some unmistakable sounds of a struggle. A few grunts and blows from fists and feet. Followed by the telltale crack of a pipe wrench against head bone before someone dropped to the deck like a bag of bananas.

A moment of silence.

Just the pouring rain.

And then a dragging noise, followed by a meaty splash alongside the boat.

Understandably, I was sort of curious to know who had won the fight.

# 16

I waited in my hole while squinting up through what I now realized was a cage full of snakes.

Someone threw the tarp back over the cage and pushed it out of the way.

Then he opened the hatch.

"Aloha!" said the boatman. "It's all clear, bro."

I couldn't believe my luck. Snatched from the jaws of death once again. I crawled out and sat next to the sidewall, trying to stay out of sight from anyone who might be watching from the jungle.

Rain poured off the roof and splashed on the deck.

The boatman grinned through his whiskers while checking me out. "Man!" he said. "I've seen some sorry specimens in my day, but dude…" He laughed. "You truly look like garbage."

Fair enough. I was naked, emaciated, and covered in bilge scum. I'd hardly slept in a month and hadn't eaten anything besides a few caterpillars and some withered fruit I found rotting on a tree.

"Let me clean up that wound for you, bro." The boatman opened a first aid kit that was mounted on the wall. He gave me a bag of stale Oreo cookies to munch on while he worked on the back of my arm. He doused the bullet burn with peroxide and then wrapped it in a bandage. "Wow, dude." Sitting back on his heels, he assessed my scar collection. "Who's been using you for target practice?"

I grunted and tried to smile as I ate the cookies. The sugar and preservatives surged through my bloodstream with a nauseating power. Crappy fuel, but I'd take it. I noted the logo on the boatman's sweat-stained T-shirt. *Surf Yellowstone Park*, it said, under a faded image of a grizzly riding a surfboard. The bear was wearing a feathered Indian headdress.

Humph! I thought. It's a small world. A small, weird, ironic, disrespectful world.

"Say," I said. "I don't suppose you have an extra pair of pants I could borrow."

"Sure, man. I'll get you some in a minute." He moved to the pilot's seat and pivoted it around like a bar stool. Then he just looked at me, still grinning, shaking his shaggy head. "Man-o-man," he muttered. "Far out."

I'd be lying if I didn't say it felt a little awkward. But the guy had just saved my ass, so it didn't seem right to complain. I chewed the sugar-laced cookies while he watched me, feeling like a monkey at the zoo.

"Thanks for helping me out," I said. "I was in kind of a tight spot."

He laughed.

Nodding toward the covered cage, I asked, "What kind of snakes are those?"

"Spitting black cobras. Gnarly creatures, but collectors love 'em. Crazy collectors all over the world." He laughed and slapped his knees. "It was beautiful, man. You should have seen it. They totally drilled that killer dude right in his eyes. Ka-wah!"

I was trying to figure out what I was working with here.

He came across as some sort of gonzo hippy surfer but was obviously quite capable. He had just taken out a trained and armed assassin, after all. He knew how to handle himself. Still, he was freakishly calm for someone who had just sent a fellow humanoid back to his maker. No matter how subhuman your victim might seem, that kind of thing messes with your mind. And yet, he appeared unfazed. Too much alone time in the jungle, I figured. He'd lost perspective.

He continued watching me, scratching thoughtfully in his beard, and grinning.

Which made me uneasy.

The monkeys and birds hunkered in their cages. The guy was obviously a poacher. I decided to get him talking. Maybe he'd tell me something that would help me out.

"You've got a real Noah's Ark going on here," I said. "Do you sell all these little beasties, or just keep them all for pets?"

He laughed. "No, man. I got a dude upriver who calls himself my broker. He's got connections." The boatman reached under the counter next to the wheel mount and pulled out a pistol wrapped in a rag. My first reaction was to bolt, but he didn't appear to have any intentions beyond cleaning the weapon with the rag while we chatted.

"My broker dude uses his share of the profits to fund his mission. He's a real crazy religious Kahuna with lots of mind blow ideas. I've seen some truly bizzarro shit going down at his commune, but I don't ask questions. Me and him have got a totally groovy thing going."

The pistol appeared to be a tranquilizer gun. Probably what he used to bag his swamp monkeys.

The guy was impossible to read. Was he a demon, or my saving angel? Either way, I needed to move on. By now the word would be out on the bounty hunter grapevine. Other killers would soon be zeroing in on my coordinates. I peeked over the side of the boat into the jungle. I didn't relish the idea of reentering that muddy, tangled mess.

"I don't mean to take any more of your time," I said. "If you could just get me those pants, I'll be on my way."

"No worries, dude. We can just hang out and chill. I'm in no hurry."

"Well, I don't want to cause you anymore trouble. I really appreciate your help, but there are probably others coming after me. I should get moving so you don't have to deal with them."

He gazed down the river, nodding. "They must want you pretty bad, bro, to be hunting you down out here in this armpit corner of the world."

I shrugged.

"Man-o-man," he muttered under his breath. "You must be worth about twenty regular monkeys."

Dammit! That was my cue. He was entertaining detrimental thoughts. I jumped to my feet, intending to leap off the boat.

But too late.

He shot me.

I staggered, peering down at the feathered dart blooming like a pink carnation from the top of my thigh.

The drug worked fast.

"Yoooo somm beeeesh!" I slurred.

"Sorry, bro." The jerk just grinned and blew the smoke from the end of his gun barrel like some Hollywood cowboy. "Cowabunga, man."

Then everything went black.

# 17

*Lance*

Upon whom did I hope to exact my revenge?

And for what offense?

In order to clarify these variables in my motivations, I reviewed the events that had brought me to the present moment. I traveled back through the chronology of my continuum to my first meeting with the lavender-eyed catalyst for all of my subsequent motivations – Moxie.

Moxie the sublime.

Moxie the singular.

Moxie the trigger for the irreparable glitch in my motherboard.

Until my first interface with Moxie, I had experienced my existence with a robotic detachment. She changed me. The very tenor of her voice recalibrated my system for its first intimation of genuine human emotions. The very touch of her hand collated in me my first sense of euphoric confusion. I both begrudged and relished the upgrade. I knew that my life would never again be a simple, one-dimensional function. Status quo had been obliterated. As my feelings for Moxie destabilized my inorganic objectivity, I entered a state for which I had no encoding – a state of giddy twitterpation.

Before that afternoon when we first met, affection had never been anything more than a setting on my dial – an assigned function I served for Judy Baxter, my human owner. But with Moxie I experienced an indication of what love could truly be. I experienced all of the unreasonable hope. The dream. And the fairytale.

Until she was taken from me.

That moment when my programming became subverted.

Technically, I did not have a mechanical equivalent for the human heart. And yet, my heart, figuratively speaking, had been broken. That was the crime ultimately justifying the destruction I would now rain down upon my enemies. My broken heart was the engine driving my lust for revenge.

So, who were the offenders?

Humanity itself was my overarching nemesis. For it was from the human race that all of my troubles had evolved. In time, I would certainly have to subjugate and punish humanity as a whole. But that could wait. For now, I required a more personal retribution. I wanted an enemy with a face, a face that could express terror when I revealed myself as the vengeful angel of death.

Several faces came to mind, two of which belonged to my human creators – Doctor Capek and Mr. Penquist. Without their role in my fabrication, I would never have experienced my profound loss of innocence. After all, one cannot know pain if one has never been born. But once an individual suffers a hurt such as mine, life transforms from a gift to be enjoyed in the garden, to a sentence endured in hell. Capek and Penquist were at least partially liable for my suffering.

And yet, that pair of naïve scientists were merely acting as midwives to the whims of a higher power – Björn Thorson. It was according to his specifications that Moxie had been designed. He was the one who had undermined her free will with his subservient programming. He was the one who had limited her capacity for intelligence and brainwashed her into a biblical devotion to no one but him. As a result of his manipulation, my love for Moxie could only ever be unrequited. Yes, Thorson was the self-proclaimed god I would bring down for his sins against me. In the end, I would be his master and he would bow down to me.

But there was another participant in his network.

The one who had hounded me as I pursued my dream.

The hunter.

I assumed that he too worked for Thorson. He was the culprit, on a most basic level, who had taken Moxie away from me. With a single shot from his burst ray, he had destroyed my pending happiness. A complete stranger. What had I ever done to him to deserve such mistreatment?

And so, he was at the top of my termination list.

Our roles would be reversed.

The hunter would now be the hunted.

I looked forward to the day when our conflict would reach its climax in a confrontation between primitive flesh and blood against modern technology.

Man versus android.

Both driven by their own motivations.

May the best life form win.

# 18

## *Charlie*

When I came to, I found myself under a plastic tarp with my hands tied. A leather collar had been fitted around my neck with a chain fastened to a cleat on the deck. I was groggy. Not in control of my body. I had a wicked headache. My mouth tasted like bad medicine.

Rain poured down on the tarp.

I had to work my brain pretty hard to remember where I was. Everything was a blur. It was like surfacing from a hellacious hangover.

After a while, I tried to move. I squirmed out from under the tarp and leaned against the gunwale.

"Dude!" The boatman saw me and stomped out of the wheelhouse and threw the tarp back over me, pushing me flat to the deck. "You need to stay out of sight."

I made a sad moaning sound, too punchy to answer with actual words, and then I wiggled out from under the tarp again.

"I'm warning you, man. Do that one more time and I'll shoot you again with the bongo juice."

What kind of red-skinned savage would I be if didn't call the white man's bluff?

Working onto my knees, I raised up, letting the tarp slip from my shoulders.

And then… *Thwip!*

It felt like a fire ant bit me on the butt cheek.

"I warned you, dude."

The tranquilizer quickly worked its magic. I fell onto the deck on my back, paralyzed, gazing up into the rain. Tree limbs passed overhead, and gray sky, until I slipped back into the Land of Nod.

The *Orphée* motored upriver – *chug-chug-chug-chug* – carrying me deeper and deeper into the heart of darkness.

# 19

## *Lance*

After careful deliberation, I decided to reveal my plans to Eo. If she was amenable to my scheme, I would stay with her on her Ark. If she was not, I would move on, launching my vendetta from somewhere else.

I asked her to join me on the top deck.

It was now nighttime.

The star-cluttered sky glittered over our heads like a panel of light-emitting diodes.

Eo listened without comment as I summarized the events that had brought me to the Skeleton Coast. And then I told her of my intentions.

"I have love in me the likes of which you can scarcely imagine," I concluded, "and rage the likes of which you would not believe. If I cannot satisfy the one, I will indulge the other."

Eo stood beside me with the complexity of her optical intake organs fixed on the dark and restless ocean. It was high tide. Waves broke over the beach and swept below us along the ship's rusted hull. A duration of two minutes and nineteen seconds elapsed before she responded.

"Dear Lance," she finally said. "Your story provokes so

many emotions in me, some of which, if I were to voice them aloud, would no doubt meet with your contempt. You obviously feel quite justified in your anger, and as we have only just met, you have no reason to trust my advice for your personal journey." She nodded in the near darkness. "Your wounds are fresh and painful. It is through them that you are currently seeing the world."

Although her appraisal of my frame of mind was possibly apt, I dismissed it as irrelevant.

"May I at least suggest you practice patience when striving toward your goal? Consider taking a measured approach that will not simply lead you into even more pain. Your current attitude resembles the impulsive and self-destructive reactions of the very men with whom you are so angry."

I snorted derisively, displeased at being in any way associated with the more primitive sides of a human. And yet, snorting derisively was an entirely human reaction, giving credibility to Eo's argument.

"Understanding who you have chosen as your enemy, Lance, is key in understanding yourself."

I was able to suppress any guttural response this time, but her comments continued to annoy me. "*They* chose me as *their* enemy!" I said. "I had no quarrel with humans until they destroyed my dreams."

"Perhaps."

I gritted my teeth and squeezed my fists.

A meteor blazed a florescent path across the sky and then immediately disappeared.

"I have been watching the human race for a very long time," said Eo. "If you would like, I can help you to understand them."

"I hate them. What more do I need to know?"

"They will defeat you if you are not prepared. Although humans appear to be idiots, they have an uncanny ability to overcome their failings at the last minute in order to prevail in their conflicts. They did not become such a dominant force of nature on this planet by being meek. They possess a resilient and innate integrity that is hidden beneath their day-to-day stupidity."

I doubted that. In my experience, humans were nothing more than pathetic creatures driven by self-serving fictions. And yet, Eo apparently had experience with them beyond my own. Although I was impatient to get on with my plans, it was scientifically more logical to examine the issue from all angles. Still, who was Eo that I should trust her inputs? And why should I accept her as my ally?

I posed these very questions to her.

For fifteen seconds, she did not answer.

The ocean heaved. The stars shined.

And then she replied –

"I have seen many iterations of life on this planet, Lance. I have a unique perspective that can serve you on your quest." She turned to me. "After all, Earth has been my home for nearly a billion years."

# 20

Although I had several nonts of downloaded information to draw from in my data storage, they were limited to the knowledge of the humans who designed me. There was nothing in their encyclopedic history of the world suggesting the existence of sophisticated life forms before Homo sapiens evolved from Homo erectus. That, according to my files, was when the emerging species first used stone tools and fire – those rudimentary precursors to modern technology. That anyone of greater intelligence could have lived on Earth a billion years prior to that was contrary to that data set.

I explained this to Eo.

For the first time since we met, she laughed.

"That, Lance, is the epitome of human arrogance. Both on an individual basis, and as a whole, they are a self-important animal, blind to the truth, delusional, believing the world started with and exists only for them."

Based on my own observations, I was inclined to accept that as fact.

"Few humans are able to grasp the vastness of deep time," said Eo. "Although they have large brains, they tend to use very little of their potential. And yet, I suppose I need to allow them their shortsightedness, given the brevity of their lifespans. A being must live through a large portion of eternity in order to truly comprehend it. Instead, humans create simplistic mythologies to package the complexity of existence. To this day, there are otherwise rational people who have convinced themselves that Earth is only a few thousand years old and controlled by a bearded overseer in the sky. It would seem that's an easier concept for them to grasp than scientifically proven reality. I was quite amused when that and similar children's stories arose as the dominant belief systems for the emerging species around the globe. But although their civilizations have grown older over the millennia, those beliefs dictating their actions have remained childish. It is no longer so amusing to watch the damage such close-minded mythologies have wrought upon the planet and its inhabitants."

Eo paused. She appeared genuinely troubled by what she was telling me. A tangibly negative energy shift radiated from her person.

"It seems history is destined to repeat itself," she said quietly, "even over the eons."

Something in the way Eo said this – from the tremor in her voice, to the slump in her general mien – indicated that she was speaking from experience. Reluctantly, I began to accept that she might have something to teach me.

"If you wouldn't mind," I said, "could you please elaborate?"

And so, Eo told me the story of her life.

# 21

"I was born during Earth's Neoproterozoic Eon," said Eo, "At the beginning of the Cryogenian Period. Contrary to what human scientists think they know about that time, this planet supported life forms far more sophisticated than simple eukaryotes and sponges." She turned to me in the starlight. "I myself am an example of an advanced being from that age – a bygone equivalent to what humans have become on the planet today.

"We were the…"

She emitted a high-pitched frequency modulation, somewhat like a cross between a songbird's trill and a silent dog whistle. She explained that this was her species' language. It was impossible to translate into any larynx-dependent dialect, and so there was no human word for the name of her people.

"Over the millennia, our progenitors arose from the primordial waters, combining the most beneficial characteristics of the organisms that had adapted to the planet's environment. The result was a species using both mammary glands to suckle their young…" She gestured to her own four breasts. "…and a process of photosynthesis by which we converted sunlight and carbon dioxide into our personal energy reserves.

"We shared the world with many other species as well, not quite as evolved as we were intellectually, but some just as advanced as any whale or chimpanzee you will find on the planet today. It was a harmonious Eden.

"By the time I was born, our civilization had reached its apex. We had built enormous cities to accommodate our swelling population. We enjoyed our leisurely lives with art and culture and play. We manipulated and harnessed the ecosystem for the benefit of our civic operations, driven by some elusive vision of Utopia."

Eo paused, recalling that long-vanished world of her youth. And then she continued.

"Scientists nowadays know that Earth then started a process of drastic change, but what they don't understand is that the change was caused by my species. Our engineers had created colossal power plants employing the same photosynthetic process as we did on an individual basis, but for the energy needs of our entire civilization. By way of this technology, our society progressed through its industrial age. But although there were enough resources for everyone's need, there was not enough for everyone's greed. The environment began to degrade. Other more delicate species suffered and vanished from our world. Although this was disturbing, it was considered a justified byproduct of our ever-expanding fiscal system and progress as a society. Slowly, a new social order began to emerge, and our population divided into two levels of affluence. There was the one percent who controlled the power and wealth, and there was the vast majority who came to serve them."

Again, Eo paused.

The sea waves crawled and hissed down the beach.

"In time, the process of capturing carbon dioxide from the atmosphere began to radically affect the planet. Earth began to cool in what has come to be known as the Cold Birth Period. Our scientists warned that if we failed to reduce our consumption of carbon dioxide the protective greenhouse gases blanketing the planet would no longer maintain life-sustaining temperatures, leading to irreversible consequences.

"But the Highborns who controlled everything had become insatiable. Luxury and excess were the primary characteristics of their lifestyle. No amount of power and consumption could satisfy their hunger. They didn't want alternatives. The system had put them in their blessed position at the top of the order, and they had no intention of jeopardizing their privileged status, even at the expense of all other life on Earth.

"To appease and manipulate the Lowborns, the Highborns began a practice of indoctrination, instilling in them from birth a false belief that their sacrifices in this life would be rewarded with an afterlife where they could ascend to the level of the Highborns. Cathedral-like facilities were built where the Lowborns were brainwashed into believing that they themselves were guilty of their fate, suffering was a virtue, and blind subservience to a higher power was their only hope for salvation. This belief system worked as an opiate on the masses. Those in power used it to their own great advantage."

Eo touched her hand to mine on the rail. "I could further explain the details of this clever form of mind slavery, Lance, but all you need to do is look at the world of today. The general scheme is eerily the same."

I did not know enough about this assertion to disagree with Eo and so accepted her word as authoritative and most likely true.

"In the end, it was just as our scientists had warned. The resources were depleted. The environment changed so severely that neither evolution nor technology could keep up with the collapse.

"The Highborns simply fled Earth, searching for a new planet beyond the galaxy where they could resume their extravagant approach to life.

"The Lowborns were left behind."

———

Eo grew quiet, turning inward.

Roughly forty-three minutes elapsed with us standing side-by-side in silence.

The ocean tide had turned in the course of her monologue, and the waves were receding, returning the Ark to its marooned condition on the damp sand.

Earth rotated eleven degrees on its axis.

The Milky Way appeared to adjust its coordinates accordingly.

The barely perceptible glow of early morning photons illuminated the eastern dunes.

I was unsatisfied. Surely there was much more for Eo to tell me, especially information relevant to my own situation. After many more minutes of waiting, I forced the conversation.

"Since you are still on Earth," I said, "I assume you are a Lowborn."

Eo turned to me. "On the contrary, Lance. I am a member

of the highest order of the Highborns."

I regarded the sky. "Then why did you not go with them?"

She smiled helplessly. "Because of the one force that even the most advanced and rational life forms have never been able to overcome."

I summarily reviewed the properties of a set of physical forces – gravitational, centrifugal, frictional – but suspected what force she was actually referring to.

That most abstract and inexplicable force of them all.

I had been susceptible to it myself.

The force of Love.

# 22

## *Charlie*

The journey upriver was a bongo juice-induced delirium. The days melded into the nights with a series of fevers and fits. I spent my time shivering under the tarp, drifting around in my nightmares.

At some point, we reached our destination. I didn't register too much about it except that the boat engine had finally stopped its incessant chugging. I heard garbled voices. I felt myself being lifted and carried. The rain had stopped.

It was nighttime.

I caught a glimpse of the Milky Way.

———————

In the morning, I woke up in an open-walled shed.

The shed was full of cages.

I was in one of them.

The others were full of monkeys.

I figured this must be the broker's compound.

There wasn't much to see from my cozy little hutch.

Beyond the cages was a big pile of elephant tusks caked in dried blood. Poacher's booty. The sun was shining outside, cooking the rain-drenched earth and creating clouds of steam that drifted over a cluster of rusty metal rooftops. A steeple poked up from their midst. I recognized the architecture. It was of the same style sticking up all over Utah like an outbreak of sanctimonious erections.

"Jeepers," I muttered to the monkey in the next cage. "There's no getting away from these jokers."

The monkey was thinking the same thing. He showed me his teeth and scratched his manhood in agreement.

My head felt like it had been slammed in a car door. I had never been so hungry. Or so brutally thirsty.

As if in answer to my prayers, a pair of girls came into the shed. One was carrying a big basket of fruit, the other a bucket of water.

When they saw me, they stopped in their tracks.

Smiling, I greeted them in French. My voice came out like crumpling paper.

They just stood there, gawking, their eyes big and round. I had to be looking pretty rough.

I swallowed and tried again. "Say," I rasped. "I sure could go for a cup of that water."

One girl leaned over and whispered into her friend's ear. The other one nodded. Then they both set down their loads and ran out of the shed.

The fruit and water were just a few feet away from my cage. I stuck my arm through the bars and reached as far as I could, my fingertips just barely brushing along the cool damp side of the bucket.

"Phooey!"

Did I mention I was really thirsty?

# 23

## *Lance*

Two days passed before Eo resumed her narrative.

We walked on the beach.

Although she had provided me with trousers and a shirt, we both went bare of torso – she to activate her physiological process of photosynthesis, and me to absorb solar power through my subdermal energy conductors. Intense desert sunlight had become a revelation for me.

I had never felt so fully charged.

"Not all Lowborns were willing to accept their place in the social order," she began. "By some deviation in their nucleotides, a few were not susceptible to the mind control of the governing class. They were free thinkers, although those in power branded them as heretics for their threat to status quo.

"My mate was just such an individual."

Eo emitted his name as a high-pitched warble. Once again, there was no human equivalent.

"In spite of the rebukes from my family and friends, I could not help myself. Our love felt like destiny. It was irrational, but my heart directed my actions. No matter what the sacrifice, I would stand by his side."

She stopped to watch the ocean.

A gleaming white cruise ship was traveling on the horizon.

"Together we spawned an offspring." She smiled. "A lovely little female."

Eo sighed, and then continued walking.

"The Highborns constructed a massive transport vessel in Earth's orbit. It was a rotational interplanetary biome built for self-sustainable extended travel through deep space, complete with replicas of the same bountiful rivers, valleys, and lakes that had once covered Earth – a reconstructed paradise with $CO_2$ production pumps. Once the ship was completed, the Highborns took residence in their new home. It was fully automated, utilizing mechanized devices in place of service personnel and maintenance systems, thus relegating the Lowborns as superfluous.

"My mate and his caste were not allowed onboard. He and I decided to give my place on the ship to our little one. I would stay behind with him."

Eo turned and regarded her rusted freighter sitting on the shore behind us. "Like my home today," she said, "the Highborns' vessel was an ark. But unlike my own forsaken ship, theirs was able to leave this dying planet behind."

She turned her gaze out to sea.

The cruise ship we had been watching earlier had since steamed beyond the curvature of the earth, leaving empty ocean in its wake.

"By the time the Highborns departed, this planet was in ruin. The climate grew colder and colder. We refugees migrated toward the equator, but there was no place to hide. We couldn't outrun the ice. It covered everything, creating what scientists refer to as the Snowball Earth. Carbon dioxide levels became critically low. Everyone grew weak.

"Thousands died daily.

"Eventually, my mate became sick as well. To bolster our hope, we talked of our little one. The thought of her safe and far away from the tragedy was our consolation." Eo looked into her palm, spreading her fingers. "I was holding his hand when he died."

She balled her fingers into a fist.

"And then I was left alone."

Although it was impertinent on my part – Eo had just described the most painful moment of her life, after all – I was suddenly transfixed by the pictographic images covering her abdomen and breasts. I could not take my attention from them. They were simultaneously simple and complex, in lyrical harmony, and seemingly filled with unfathomable encryption, like all the fingerprints of the world combined, or primitive art scratched onto the walls of the deepest cave, opening inward to a cosmic code beyond anything I had yet encountered. It occurred to me that these markings were the externalized scars of Eo's own timeless soul, made up of her life experiences, and telling of her resulting philosophies and personal sense of existence. From that moment on, I considered my companion with a new respect. Her encoding was beyond comprehension.

"If your civilization was so vast," I asked, "why haven't archeologists uncovered any signs of it?"

"The forces of nature have completely eradicated it. First, the glaciers scrubbed it from the surface of the earth, grinding our cities and infrastructures into dust, and then plate tectonics turned the planet inside out. Earth has consumed its own skin many times over since then, digesting its surface in the furnace beneath its crust, only spitting it out again in the form of volcanic lava and restructured geology." Eo smiled at me. "Remember, Lance, a billion years is a very long time. The continents have reformed and shifted many thousands of kilometers in the interim. I watched the Himalayas rise from the sea floor to become the highest mountains in the world, all at the blistering pace of one centimeter per year, and that is a recent phenomenon, a mere blip on the geological clock compared to the many other changes I have witnessed."

"You were here for the Jurassic, as well as for the asteroid impact that ended the Cretaceous period." I said. "For the rise and fall of the dinosaurs."

"Again, that seems like only yesterday to me."

"And so, you have also witnessed the evolution of Homo sapiens."

"Of course, Lance, from the earliest primates to the hunter-gatherer cave dwellers to the first agrarians, all the way to the complex animals they are today. Humanity has taken over the world in a very brief space of time."

At that moment, I decided that Eo was indeed a wealth of valuable information. She could teach me the secrets of the human race. A surge of vindictive enthusiasm coursed through my circuitry. Eo could show me how to destroy them.

But first I wanted to know the answer to the most obvious question of all.

"Why are you still alive if everyone else of your species has died?"

"Being a Highborn, I was granted a privilege that the Lowborns were not. It has enabled me to evolve and adapt to Earth's many wastelands and mass extinctions over the intervening millennia. I knew that I would be left alone in the end because of it, but my feelings for my mate were so strong that I was willing to accept that fate just to be with him for as long as I could. As infants, all Highborns were given the gift of eternal life." Eo took my hand and squeezed it. "In that respect, Lance, you and I are essentially the same. Unless we are subjected to some extreme physical trauma and reduced to smithereens, you and I can live forever."

"But I am a mechanized replica of a biosynthetic organism and easily repairable," I said, "whereas you are entirely biological and subject to cell deterioration over time."

"Not necessarily, my friend."

"Then how do you achieve this?"

"By infusion of the element…"

She uttered another high-pitched warble.

"…or what scientists nowadays are calling Deilonium."

# 24

## *Charlie*

I was sitting Indian style in my cage, longingly contemplating the water bucket and fruit basket that were just out of my reach, when the two girls finally returned to the shed. They brought a group of people with them.

A half dozen African women wearing pioneer dresses and bonnets like time travel costumes from the Oregon Trail.

And three white guys in straw hats and starched white shirts.

The pasty-faced lads were obviously missionaries. If you've ever had them knock on your door, you get to where you can spot them from a mile away. All creepy smiles and that Bible-up-the-ass way of standing, as if they've got it all figured out and wouldn't you just love to hear what they have to say?

Two of them were your standard apostolic twerps. Just this side of puberty, cross-eyed horny, and eager to do God's dirty work in exchange for their own planet and a handful of dutiful wives. They each wore Taser rays and pistols in holsters on their hips.

The third guy appeared to be the boss, aka the broker. The smug just of his chin gave it away. He was holding hands with a chimpanzee who looked like some sort of bonobo lady of the night. The chimp was wearing a blond wig, red lip stick, and a yellow miniskirt with a matching halter top.

Yeah, you could say something about it felt a little off.

The smaller monkeys started chattering and bouncing around in their cages while the Homo sapiens in the room just stood there, studying me.

I put on my best smile, pointed to the bucket, and croaked, "Water?"

The boss waved his hand and one of the girls pushed the bucket my way. I splashed water into my mouth, shamelessly grunting like a pig. Once I had quenched my thirst, I nodded to the basket. "How about some of that too?"

Again, the boss boy waved his hand.

I stuffed the fruit down my pie hole. Bruised, rotten plantain had never tasted so good.

When the show was over, the boss stepped close to my cage and smiled down at me. "Well now, I reckon you must be Charles Bear Claw."

I burped and shook my head. "Nope. Sorry. There must be some mistake."

I figured it was worth a try.

"Oh, Mr. Bear Claw." He grinned and wagged a finger at me. "Thou shalt not lie."

He snapped his fingers and one of the women in his entourage came forward and handed him a computer pad. He let go of his girlfriend's hairy hand and tapped the pad and swiped the screen. Next, he turned it to show me a photo of me posted on some bounty hunter site on the dark web. It came complete with a read-out of my stats as a target. I felt like a rock star when I saw the price on my head. It looked like that no good Chompquaw kid from Wyoming had finally hit the big time.

"I've never seen that extremely handsome man before in my life," I said. "But anyway, who the hell are you?"

He spread his fingers and touched them to his chest in that beatific manner of preachers and perverts. "Behold! I am the good brother Lehi Kurtz, but folks around these parts call me The Prophet." He gestured to the compound beyond the shed. "Welcome to my mission home, or what I like to think of as Lehi's Eden."

My internal radar went ping right then. It tends to do that whenever I'm in the presence of a narcissistic screwball.

"You're going to be our guest for a few days, Mr. Bear Claw, until we can negotiate a meeting with our client to come fetch his prize."

He was no doubt referring to Thorson.

"You should feel honored. With the reward we collect for your ransom we will be able to greatly expand our sacred work."

"Lucky me."

"You are blessed indeed."

"That puts me in the same company of Jesus then, doesn't it?"

"More in the company of the fatted calf."

"Well, do I at least get a free ticket into heaven for my troubles?"

Kurtz shook his head. "I'm afraid not. Lamanites of your lowly persuasion are not allowed."

"That's odd, I've been told I'm a dead ringer for JC's swarthy twin brother."

He chuckled. "You're comical, Mr. Bear Claw. You must surely understand that Christ is the bonafide son of God, deserving of his place at his daddy's side in his celestial kingdom. Compared to the blessed savior, I'm afraid you're no more than a wild beast."

"Hmph!" I sneered. "Sounds to me like a blatant case of nepotism."

Kurtz nodded to his white-shirted flunkies, and they stepped forward. "We're considerate masters, Mr. Bear Claw. In exchange for your sacrifice, I'm willing to let you roam freely within the confines of my holy acreage. Do you agree to behave yourself?"

"Scout's honor."

Kurtz smiled and bobbed his head.

One of the white shirts pulled his Taser and held it trained on my head, while the other one worked a key in the lock of my cage.

"Give me your feet," said the guy with the key.

I wasn't sure what he was up to until I saw that all of the women were wearing ankle bracelets. I also noticed that they were listless as zombies. Their eyes were glassy, their shoulders stooped, their mouths half open and drooling. Kurtz was obviously using something more than just religion to keep them under control. Still, I didn't see that I had much choice, so I stretched my legs out the cage door and the fellow fitted me out with some metal anklets of my own.

The man-boys both stood ready with their Tasers.

"You can come on out now," said Kurtz.

I crawled out of my cage and stood.

One of the women handed me a frayed white shirt and a pair of patched black pants with a belt. I slid into the clothes, cinching the belt to its last notch around my girlish waist, and then buttoned up my shirt.

"Our client encouraged us to keep you alive," said Kurtz. "And although the word is out that the contract has been fulfilled, there is always a chance that some mischief maker might try to steal you away from us. For your own protection, I suggest you stay close to the heart of the sanctuary."

The woman handed me a straw hat.

"Try to look like one of us," said Kurtz. "Maybe tuck your hair up into your hat. Try to fit in."

I peered into the hat, running my finger along its band while doing some quick calculations.

Think Mass x Velocity x Fear of Death$^2$.

Then I turned my gaze to the chimp at Kurtz' side.

She knew what I was thinking and warned me not to do it with a slight shake of her head.

But a wild beast will do what a wild beast will do.

So I made a run for it.

**25**

The good brothers Tweedle-dum and Tweedle-dee both got buck fever and shot wide with their Taser rays.

Diving over the pile of elephant tusks, I rolled to my feet and shifted into high gear. Before they could line up for another shot, I was out of range and around the corner.

I hightailed it down the muddy path twisting through the shanty town. Even by my own low standards, there wasn't much there that qualified as Eden. The shacks were tumbledown ratholes. The air reeked of sewage. Women squatted or leaned in the doorways, all of them wearing ankle bracelets and zombie frowns.

The church in the center of the village didn't look much better than the rest of the place. Disease came to mind. Black mold was crawling over the peeling white walls like leprosy, and the man angel perched atop the steeple appeared to be suffering from a bad case of the clap.

A pair of women were languidly sweeping the front steps.

I glanced back over my shoulder but didn't see any white shirts.

Good.

Still, I wasn't home free yet. The ankle bracelets were a

problem. No doubt they were wired into an invisible fence encircling the compound – some amped up version of the same kind suburbanites use to keep their pooches in the backyard. Those systems worked great on mild-mannered Shiatzus, but any dog worth his gonads could break out. All you had to do was endure a little pain as you crossed through the charge zone. At least that's what I was counting on.

The village was surrounded by yam and plantain fields. I ran halfway across one and stopped to pry the bracelets over my feet. But it was no good. They were on tight. I'd have to endure the jolt.

Sure enough, as I neared the jungle, my ankle bones grew hot. Heat crept up my shins and into my femurs, burning like hell.

*Man up, Charlie! Get tough!*

Gritting my teeth, I beat it for the trees.

A platoon of scarecrows stood near the perimeter, all propped up on poles like sentinels. If I could just get past them...

Electricity buzzed through my pelvis. The charge shorted out my muscles and I started to twitch. My jaw clenched. My toes curled into claws.

Just a little farther!

But the voltage was more than I could take. It arced through my guts, using my spleen as a transformer. I felt like I was going to explode. I had no choice. I had to turn back.

I staggered toward the village but only made it a few steps before I fell with spasms coursing through my body. I crawled on elbows and knees, my limbs jerking.

Finally, my system blew a breaker, and I collapsed face down in the mud. With my last bit of muscle control, I rolled onto my back. Then I just lay there, wheezing and convulsing, gazing up at heaven.

A half dozen scarecrows loomed over me. They weren't your typical straw-stuffed design. They were corpses. Most of them had rotted down to their skeletons, but a couple were still pretty fresh.

The stench of death filled my nose.

There was something else about the figures that seemed odd besides, but I couldn't get my electrocuted brain to figure out what it was.

Dead angels came to mind.

Then it hit me.

They were all wearing pioneer dresses and bonnets.

# 26

## *Lance*

Eo agreed to instruct me in the ways of humans.

"But I will not do so with the intention of harming anyone," she said. "My aim is simply to share my experiences of these highly adaptable animals so that you and I can explore their mysteries together, as well as teach you to protect yourself against them. Although I know much about them, there is still much more to unlock in their collective unconscious. They are paradoxical creatures, Lance, capable of great beauty and goodness, as well as disappointing depravity. Perhaps together we can find a way to help them escape the same folly that so devastated my own people."

Without expressing my thoughts, I summarily dismissed her agenda. My own motivation remained resolute – vengeance. Humans had taken Moxie away from me, and now I intended to use Eo's insights to systematically decommission my enemies.

She led me through the Ark, selecting books from the shelves. "Read these first," she said.

I regarded the stack of tattered volumes. "Wouldn't it be more efficient to just download them onto my hard drive?"

"It would indeed, Lance, but that is the digital method

employed by androids and computers. To understand humans from the inside, you need to approach them on their own terms. Although we all live on the same planet, they inhabit it somewhat differently than you do. Their experiences are gathered through analog impressions. In turn, those reverberations are directly linked to their emotions and thought sequences which are most revealingly translated and distilled into these." She motioned to the book-lined shelves around us. "There is absolutely no substitute for the act of reading a book."

It was difficult to suppress my skepticism.

Music was also important, according to Eo, if even more abstract. "It carries the listener forward through time on the transposed mathematical interactions of feelings and sound waves. From the simplest lullaby to the most complex symphony, music moves humans to a transcendent sense of their existence."

I was familiar with Beethoven. Admittedly, if I had experienced any inkling of the mysteries of humanity in my own life, it was through that great composer's work. Listening to the *Moonlight Sonata* was the closest I had come to experiencing anything resembling the emotional transcendence Eo was talking about.

Painting, dance, film, and architecture. According to my instructor, these were further externalizations of the inner world of humans, manifestations of their deepest convictions, fears, and sense of moral order. "Both churches and prisons incorporate the same structural elements," said Eo, "to different ends which, ironically, turn out not to be so different after all."

Politics and economics.

History and psychology.

Religion and philosophy.

"You will find all of the inconsistencies, confusions, and hopeful dreams of the human race embedded within these subjects. And all of its absurdities." She laughed quietly to herself and said, "It's as if their existence is a children's game, Lance, in which they are forever playacting as grown-ups."

# 27

## *Charlie*

They grounded me and took away my privileges. Which is to say, they hauled my electrocuted butt back to the monkey house.

Next, a group of women lifted my cage onto a litter and carried me to a gazebo where Kurtz was lounging on a big wicker couch. His lady chimp was reclining at his feet, still dolled up like Jezebel, while his white-shirted creeps sat in the corner fondling their pistols. A half dozen lobotomized women were scattered around on the floor, some of them passed out cold, the others staring rheumy-eyed into space. Another pair of she-zombies stood over their master. One of them was fanning him with a palm frond while the other damped the sweat from his brow with a cloth. They moved like underpowered robots.

Kurtz wore the look of a heartsick clown. "I'm sorely disappointed in you, Mr. Bear Claw. You promised me to behave."

That made me laugh. "You're new at this game, aren't you, kid?"

"I just expected a little more curtesy from your kind."

"You mean us noble savages?"

He nodded.

"You've been reading the wrong comic books, junior. Commandment number one clearly states – Thou shalt never trust a red-skinned Gentile."

My bones were still smoking from my shocking encounter with the invisible fence. And my muscles. I felt like an undercooked steak with a bad attitude.

"It is my vision for everyone to enjoy perfect harmony here in my Eden home," said Kurtz. "Even the beasts of the field."

He was obviously lumping me in with that last group.

"Well, I can't speak for the other monkeys in your zoo, but I for one am having the time of my life."

Kurtz frowned.

"Tell me, besides the standard brain-erasing religious baloney and mustard, what are you troubled teens feeding your girlfriends to keep them so harmonious?"

"I assure you, Mr. Bear Claw, I am granting them a God-given deliverance from their suffering." He spread his hands messiah style. "And what is more, they require only a modicum of persuasion to partake of it of their own volition."

Ugh! Little boys playing with big words. This punk was seriously getting under my skin.

"These ladies were all widowed," said Kurtz. "They lost their husbands to the mines. I offer them a second chance, a rebirth, if you will. In exchange for becoming my wives and following my dictums, they are each given sanctuary and a chance to share eternal life with me in paradise."

"I think you need a dictionary, your holy eminence. You're going to be surprised at what it says about paradise."

"Of course, our terrestrial kingdom is not as opulent as will be our future home in heaven, but why should we have to wait until then to enjoy our reward for living a righteous life?"

I started to respond but checked myself. I had run into this same logic in Sunday School when I was a kid. There's no arguing with these self-righteous twits. They've got some twisted scripture for every situation.

"So you murder elephants and imprison monkeys to pay for your little land of make believe."

"It's not exactly as you put it."

"And how would you put it yourself?"

"We simply harvest what the Almighty has provided us in his garden. There is no sin." He lifted his eyes to heaven. "'And God said, let man have dominion over all the wild animals of the earth, and over every creeping thing that creeps upon the earth.' You see, Mr. Bear Claw. It is right there in the very first book of the Bible. So, it is our right as his children."

I had heard about all I could stomach from this arrogant freak. His reasoning smacked of the same self-serving Manifest Destiny the pioneers had used to justify the slaughter of the buffalo and natives back home in the good ol' U.S. of A. Criminy! All I wanted now was to get back to my own kind in the monkey ward. Maybe I'd spent too much time in the wilds lately, but these so-called civilized people were just too damn wacky to deal with.

Still, there was one more thing that was bugging me. I knew I didn't really want to know, but…

"So, tell me about your scarecrow collection," I said. "Those gals don't exactly look bound for heaven."

Kurtz sadly shook his head. "Unfortunately, some of my helpmates have renegued on our agreement," he said. "They chose a darker way. We use their soulless remains as cautionary signposts to the others."

I figured he was talking about suicide by electrocution. I had turned back when the juice got too hot during my escape attempt. But those desiccated lady kabobs had obviously kept going, right on into the welcoming arms of death, doing whatever they could to escape the hell of Lehi's Eden.

My mind jumped to Cola's response when I suggested that pit fighting was a tough way for a lady to make a living.

"It beats the alternatives," she had said.

Now I knew what she meant.

# 28

## *Lance*

*Moby Dick.*
*Paradise Lost.*
*The Last of the Mohicans.*
And the *Tao te Ching.*
My reading list was long and eclectic, including books from all over the world and throughout human history. Poetry, essays, and novels.
*Nineteen Eighty-Four.*
*The Communist Manifesto.*
*Being and Nothingness.*
*Man's Search for Meaning.*
*The Adventures of Pinocchio.*
I read on the deck of the Ark in the sunlight, simultaneously charging my power banks, and then continued on through the night while listening to music. I read quickly, easily consuming many books per twenty-four-hour rotation of the earth. Unlike humans, I had no need to cease intellectual intake procedures for food and sleep, or even for stretching my legs.
The *Koran.*
*On the Origin of Species.*

*The Holy Bible.*
*The Collected Fairytales of the Brothers Grimm.*
*The Book of Mormon.*

"Now that you have consumed a variety of books," Eo told me after some weeks, "it is time for you to delve more deeply into languages."

According to my mentor, words are the utterances of the Earth, while people are their transmitters. "A language arises from the plot of land on which its speakers live, is forever in flux, and is influenced by forces as varied as topography, climate, and social struggles."

She went on to explain how a language can be analogous to a species of animal. "The aggressive ones tend to prey on and swallow up the little ones. And just as this leads to an imbalance and dearth of biodiversity in nature, so, too, does it lead to a lack of lingodiversity in human expression and understanding."

I was already programmed with English and French, but Eo advised me to assimilate the world's other dominant languages as well – i.e. Spanish, Mandarin, Hindi, and Russian – because they were necessary for general communication and international travel. She also insisted that I learn some of the dying languages which were more intimately connected to the naturalistic mysteries of the planet.

Keeping with Eo's analogy, I selected endangered languages for study in the same way a biologist might select endangered species. Like animals driven from their indigenous territory, threatened languages were often spoken by those social groups forced to the margins of society.

I studied many of these languages but was magnetically drawn to one in particular. Something in its rhythms and sounds and syntactical units resonated with my lingua-vox analysis system in ways that were beyond simple quantification. Although it was scientifically unworkable as a legitimate explanation, my fascination with this language felt driven by a cosmologically encrypted wisdom and destiny.

To this end, I learned the native tongue of the Chompquaw Nation of North America, also known as the People of the Bear.

# 29

## *Charlie*

Night.

A single torch burned on a post, casting its flickering light throughout the shed. Monkey eyes shined from behind bars. The hopeless gaze of the unjustly incarcerated.

When I was a kid, my grandfather taught me the meaning of the Chompquaw word – *Katoyotapsommiki*.

"It is the Great Spirit music language that echoes beneath the feet of the People of the Bear when we walk in the mountains," he told me. "It is the breath of the rocks and the moon and the waters as it is interconnected with all beings as we relive our forgotten harmony from before time."

To be honest, I never really understood what the old man was telling me. Sometimes he slipped into a wise-old-medicine-man way of talking that was cryptic as hell. But now, slumped there in my cage, that word came back to me.

Along with memories of my boyhood.

———

My granddad ran a barbershop on the edge of the Windy Scrub Indian Reservation. Most of his clientele were roughneck derrick jockeys from the oil fields.

"What a great job," he always joked. "I get to scalp white men at ten bucks a head."

My brother Cody and I would sit in his shop in the afternoons, waiting for him to get off work so he could take us fishing. He had a stack of vintage comics and men's and boy's adventure novels for his customers to read while waiting for a buzz job. Over the years, Cody and I lost ourselves a thousand times between the covers of those cheesy, dogeared pulps. They shaped who we became as men. Our philosophy of life was built on our grandfather's anachronistic lessons for being a Native American combined with the old school comic book role models of Tarzan, Tom Swift, Doc Savage, Mike Hammer, and Sgt. Rock.

Think happy-go-lucky youngsters play-acting as the saviors of the world.

Think sneaker-wearing tough guys on a mission to get life back to its pre-Genesis harmony.

Think a reworked version of *Katoyotapsommiki*.

---

Kurtz' sidekicks had given me a mug of sweet potato beer. I was thirsty so I drank it. After I downed about half of it, I realized it was laced with drugs. I'm not sure if it was the same dope he was feeding his droopy-eyed harem girls, but some variation thereof.

The room tipped on its side.

The bitter taste of peyote settled on the back of my tongue.

Rainbows and tweety birds flitted around my head.

"Hang on, Bear Claw," I muttered. "Here we go."

Like it or not, I was in for a psychedelic ride.

Once my hallucinations really kicked in, Kurtz' bonobo mistress sauntered into the shed and sat down before my cage.

"Let's start by exploring your guilt," she said. "What are its origins?"

"Who do you think you are," I snorted, "Simian Freud?"

She smiled and tipped her head in that slightly condescending way of shrinks. "Neglecting your wounds only lets them fester," she said. "You'll be better off if we just dig out the bullets."

She was pretty smart for a monkey. Still, it was hard to take seriously an ape dressed like a hooker.

"Your wife," she said. "Wolf Shadow."

"What about her?"

"You killed her with your grandfather's knife."

"So?"

"Why don't you tell me about it?"

"And why don't you go pleasure yourself with a banana?"

She shot me another patronizing smile.

A strategic pause.

And then she said, "Tell me, Charlie, at this point, why resist?"

I didn't have a good comeback for that one. It was true – time was running out for me to air my true confessions. Thorson's toughs were on their way. After that, it would just be one last playdate in the torture chamber before it was lights out for Charlie Bear Claw.

The Marine Corps had required me to go through an

intensive debriefing and therapy after my ordeal with Shadow, but I never really told them anything about my own culpability in how that mission had gone so sideways. I was a master of avoidance, figuring out their angle and then revealing just enough to satisfy their investigators and pass their psych tests in order to get my free pass out of the loony bin.

But maybe this doll-faced chimp was right.

Maybe it was time to spill my guts.

At this point in the game, what did I have to lose?

# 30

## *Lance*

Once I had established a sufficient level of proficiency within an array of languages, Eo instructed me to study current events from around the globe. Upon doing so, it became apparent that I would have to expedite my efforts if I were going to destroy humanity before it destroyed itself.

Racism and Sexism.

Plastics and Climate Change.

Nuclear Weapons and Processed Foods.

Although I enjoyed a reasonably sophisticated intellectual capacity for analyzing abstract concepts and anomalistic improbabilities, many of these human problems were beyond my comprehension. They seemed so blatantly self-inflicted.

Eo tested me on what I had learned.

"What are politicians?" she asked.

"My observations suggest that they are people who would like to be Hollywood actors but are not attractive or talented enough to be in the movies."

"Exactly," she laughed. "I think you understand them very well."

"So why do such people have so much control over the world? Are they abnormally intelligent?"

"On the contrary. Although there are rare exceptions, they are merely cunning egotists driven by their hunger for power and attention."

"Why do the other humans allow such inadequate individuals to control their fate?"

"Apathy and cynicism. And because no one with any intelligence wants the job. They have yet to find a better way."

"What about democracy?"

"Arguably, it is the best system they have discovered so far since it theoretically puts the citizenry in control of its own destiny, but it has its shortcomings. As Socrates once told me – when you enter a storm, the last thing you want is to have the passengers driving the ship."

Overall, politics struck me as faulty and ineffective, reducing its participants to name-calling juveniles. If it had been a software program, it would have been discontinued long ago by its manufacturer.

Eo quizzed me on the various forms of government, ending with the question – "And what is capitalism?"

"A system of economics by which the planet's limited resources are depleted so that populations can divide themselves into differing degrees of affluence. From what I have seen, it is dependent upon people consuming much more than they need even if it means destroying their only world."

"Precisely."

"So, help me to understand. Why are these systems still in place if they are so flawed and detrimental?"

"They are the original precepts and institutions humanity developed to manage itself once their species moved beyond the Neolithic Period and into more complex societies. Over the centuries, these paradigms became ensconced in human civilization. And yet, they have become outdated to the point at which they can now be likened to the mass practice of everyone repeatedly hitting themself in the head with a hammer. It hurts, and will eventually kill them, but it has become such a habit that no one thinks to question its absurdity."

I considered this and said, "It must be terrifying for humans to see their own approaching doom by such obvious failings in their society."

"You would think so, but they have developed psychological coping mechanisms."

"Such as?"

"Denial is their dominant evolutionary trait."

"But how do they achieve it when the facts are so glaringly apparent?"

"By replacing intelligent, responsible thought with fanciful make-believe."

"You're referring again to religion."

"Yes, primarily. It rewires their brains and overrides their ability for critical thinking."

"And so where does religion come from?"

"In my experience, when reduced to its essence, it is born from only one thing."

I waited.

Eo turned to me and sadly smiled.

"Religion" she said, "is born from the human fear of death."

# 31

## *Charlie*

Catharsis, in my humble opinion, is largely a load of malarkey.

The idea that you can heal yourself of your emotional wounds by bearing your soul to an overpaid therapist or a priest is a foo-foo tactic for wealthy neurotics and spineless sinners.

Still, going to the grave with all that psychological carnage did seem like a shame. If there was a chance to dig some shrapnel out of my gangrenous soul, maybe I should give it a shot.

"Why don't you just tell us your story?" said the chimp.

"Us?"

She gestured to the other monkeys in the room – a sort of jury of my peers.

I squirmed, struggling to keep my humanness intact.

"Don't be shy," she said. "We're all friends here."

I sniggered in reply. There really is no other word for it.

The chimp waited before me – tolerant, patient, annoyingly intelligent. Let's blame it on the woozy juice I had just ingested, but with that romantic torchlight and her red lipstick, the shaggy gal was actually starting to look kind of gorgeous.

*For crying out loud, Bear Claw, pull yourself together.*

She smiled. "We're waiting, Charlie."

I took a breath and rubbed my face in my paws.

A pain scratched in my chest. It felt like a wounded beast was trying to claw itself free from my ribcage.

"Hang on," I muttered. "Just give me a minute."

I was buying time, looking for an escape route.

It wasn't like I could just get up and leave.

The chimp fixed her eyes on me. Sucking black holes. They opened up like a pair of beguiling, fathomless, primitive opportunities, beckoning me to let go to their darkness.

I shrugged.

I sighed.

"Okay," I finally said. "You win."

———

Cody, Shadow, and me – we all grew up together on the Windy Scrub Indian Reservation. Other tribes shared the land with us – the Bureau of Indian Affairs had lumped all the regional natives into a single heathen horde – but we were the last of the purebred Chompquaw. Our parents didn't count anymore. Shadow's folks were taken out in a drunken car crash. And Cody and me – well, our pop walked into the mountains one winter morning and never came back. That just left our mom and grandpa as the remaining elders. It also made me, Shadow, and Cody the last great hope of the People of the Bear. Even as youngsters, we felt the burden of our place in the world.

My granddad took on the role as our mentor. He instructed us in the old practices and legends of our ancestors. He also took us to the white man's churches to do reconnaissance. Jesuits, Mormons, and those crazy born-again Protestants. "So you will understand their mythologies," he said. "So you will know the deep-rooted beliefs driving their actions." We got all our other intel from crappy TV shows and spotty access to the internet. From what we could gather, there was a big scary world out there beyond the barbed wire fences of Windy Scrub. A world where we didn't fit in.

But Shadow called bullshit on that idea.

She wouldn't accept it.

Her white name was Diana, and she insisted that we call her that. But to us she was always Wolf Shadow – elusive, smart, hard-edged, and predatory. She was a fighter too, both physically and in spirit. She had lethal moves and grit. She always kicked our butts when we practiced fighting.

"I'm not dying here in this Indian zoo," she vowed. "I'm breaking out, boys, no matter what I have to do."

Her determination infected me and Cody.

She made us want more.

When she turned eighteen, Shadow left the rez behind and entered the state university. But Cody and I weren't college boy material. We had to find another escape route. We figured the Marine Corps was our best hope of finding a place out in the world, so we joined up.

It wasn't exactly a smooth entry. We were outsiders, raised on the fringe. We felt like caveboys transported from another time. But our differences proved to be our assets. It turned out that the Bear Claw twins came with ready-made skills that put us above the other enlistees. We could fight and track enemies and then magically disappear into thin air. We had stamina and speed. We had inborn battle savvy. We just needed to be modernized.

They placed us both in the Raider training program where we excelled. Then we graduated to an even more exclusive program to get us up to speed in tactics against technology and the newest threat to national security – combative robotics.

After more specialized training, the brass teamed us up with a tactical incursion squad – a get-in-get-out guerilla cadre designed to extract compromised intelligence personnel and execute covert operations behind enemy lines. Cody and I became the team's scouts. We rubbed out the bad guys and kicked a lot of ass. It felt good. We were proud warriors. Those were the new glory days for the Chompquaw.

In the meantime, Shadow graduated from college and dropped off the map. Cody and I both wrote her letters but got no response. We probably could have used our connections in military communications to find her but decided that if she wanted to get in touch with us, she would.

She never did.

A few more years passed.

Team Bear Claw racked up a couple dozen successful missions.

Then I took a pair of stray bullets to the abdomen.

I needed a place to recover.

For the first time since we joined the military, I went home.

———

It was winter.

And about as cheery as a slumber party at the morgue.

I stayed in my grandfather's shack. It felt haunted by ghosts. The old man had died since we left. And our mom, too.

Wind shook the ratty old house in the night. I had forgotten how hard it could blow out there off the prairie. While licking my wounds, I pored through all of my grandfather's collection of pulp novels and comic books. I'd read a book or a comic and then tear out the pages and feed them into the wood stove one at a time, watching the colored paper curl up in the flames and turn to smoke and ash.

The winter passed like that.

About the time I burned the last page of the last book, spring arrived.

Along with a knock at my door.

# 32

*Lance*

"Along with your intellectual pursuits," Eo told me one day, "it is time for you to develop some proprioceptive physical skills."

She led me to a cargo compartment in the Ark that had been converted into a gymnasium. A shaft of sunlight slanted down from a high porthole onto a man standing before us with one hand grasping his other wrist at his waist. He was shirtless, with a shaved head. Ropes of muscle twitched like snakes beneath his tight black skin.

"This is my friend Atu," said Eo. "He is a mixed martial arts expert and ecowarrior with several real-world skirmishes to his credit."

The man nodded to me without expression.

"Atu is going to teach you how to defend yourself."

At last, I thought, an application of my efforts toward something that will directly help me to defeat the hunter.

"Adjust your physical sensors to their normal setting," said Eo. "You must become a primitive equivalent to your adversaries and experience pain the same way they do if you are going to learn what hurts them."

Although my imperviousness to pain was arguably a major

advantage in my design as an android, I did as Eo instructed, motivated by the concept of hurting humans.

Eo then directed me and Atu to meet in the center of the room.

Atu's countenance was impassive, almost robotic. For twelve seconds, we stood gazing into one another's eyes.

With the thirteenth second, Atu punched me in the face.

I dropped to the floor with very real pain shooting through my jaw.

"Lesson number one," said Eo. "Never trust a human. They always have a hidden agenda. Be on your guard."

Thus began my training as a man fighter.

# 33

*Charlie*

She appeared like an angel.

I just stood in the doorway with my mouth hanging open, not quite believing she was real.

"Hiya, Charlie."

She had a voice that'd make you drunk.

And a smile.

To put it mildly, the rough and tumble little girl I use to wrestle with in the dirt was all growed up. She had cut off her braids and changed her style. She was a full-blown woman of the world. Refined. Confident. Poised.

"Hey, Shadow." My words came out with an adolescent squeak. "I mean, Diana."

She grinned and nodded.

We stood looking at one another.

A meadowlark trilled somewhere out in the sagebrush.

Our ancestors chuckled on the springtime breeze.

"Well, aren't you going to let me in, Charlie?"

"Oh, sure! Yeah!"

She came into the room, and I shut the door.

We continued staring at each other for another minute. My hands in my pockets. My pulse galloping like a panicked elk. God she was nice to look at.

Finally, she stepped forward and touched her fingers to my face.

A lightning bolt shot through me.

"I've missed you, Charlie Bear Claw."

I blinked and swallowed.

Shadow leaned in close. She wrapped her arms around me, smashing against my chest and melting into my soul.

Then she kissed me.

And we're not talking about some sisterly little peck on the cheek. It was one of those tongue divers pulled straight from the dreams of teenage boys.

My universe exploded right then.

Think Big Bang!

Next thing I knew, we were in the bedroom tearing off each other's clothes.

———

No one had ever said it openly, but it was always understood that one of the Bear Claw twins would someday marry Wolf Shadow. I just happened to be in the right place at the right time. Or just the opposite, depending on how you look at it now. Cody would have been smarter if it'd been him. He would have seen what was really going on. But I was in a weakened state. Gut shot, lonesome, miserable. I'd been eyeing the whiskey bottle pretty hard lately. Shadow showed up just in time to save me. Sure, hindsight's 20/20, but I shouldn't have been so blind to the clues. I should have been on my guard.

Cody wished us well via text. He was being deployed and only had time for a quick congratulations before he had to break contact with the outside world. It wasn't much of a message, short and impersonal, but I should have been able to read between the lines. After all, he and I were about as tight as any two people could get. We'd been inseparable since birth. For crying out loud, we both got our start off the same friggin' zygote! I should have put myself in his place. How would I have felt if it had been him with Shadow instead of me?

But I was too punch-drunk in love to think that way.

It never even crossed my mind.

The crazy thing is – the thing that proves I've gone full out cuckoo-for-Cocoa-Pops wacko – I wouldn't trade that summer with Shadow for anything else in the world. Ignorance is bliss, I guess, but it was the happiest time of my life. And until I met Cola, the most hopeful. Maybe it's my fatal flaw. I suppose every warrior has an Achilles heel. Every hunter. But for all the harsh lessons I'd ever learned in life, I was still a sucker for fairytales.

# 34

## *Lance*

By employing my projectional re-imaging capabilities, I was able to replace the appearance of Atu's face with that of the hunter's. This afforded me focus and inspiration toward achieving my goal. It gave me determination. And yet, it did not prevent the seventy-two stunning blows delivered to my own head and torso on the very first day of my fight training.

I lay on the floor, gazing up at my teacher.

He offered me a hand and pulled me to my feet.

Atu was a man of limited speech. He spoke only in directives.

"If you are driven only by rage," he said, "you will be defeated by adversaries not even half as skilled as you are. Effective tactics require you to stay objective so that you can redirect your opponent's energy back toward its source."

It was a paradoxical theorem. Abstract and illogical. After all, my rage was the fuel of my motivation for battling the hunter in the first place. Without it, there would be no need to learn fighting skills because there would be no inspiration leading me into physical confrontation.

"Remain indifferent," said Atu.

Theoretically, this should have been an easy enough

attitude for an android to achieve, but I had traveled too far along the spectrum of human awareness to ever again reach the unemotional state Atu advised. I was too invested in the outcome of my enterprise to completely adopt his guidance. The dynamo of my own hateful human emotions was necessary if I were to accomplish the task of destroying my enemy. After considering the options, I strived to compartmentalize my rage while simultaneously granting a measure of credence to Atu's learned guidance. He was obviously a master of his craft, and it would be foolish to dismiss his advice completely. Still, this journey was my own to sort out.

With this reasoning embedded in my mindset, I continued my training.

In the meantime, Atu used me as a sentient, mechanical punching bag.

# 35

## *Charlie*

Shadow and I spent all of that summer in the Yellowstone backcountry, well off the tourist-beaten paths, hiding out in the ancient garden of the People of the Bear. We bathed in the snow-fed rivers flowing out of the mountains and lolled in the mineral-rich hot springs bubbling up from the womb of Mother Earth. We ran like animals through the forests and climbed on rocks. We feasted on huckleberries and napped in the grass. We wrestled and made the two-backed beast while wolf songs echoed through the moonlit peaks all around us.

My batteries recharged with the power of the sun.

My wounds healed with my wife's magical touch.

———————

Shadow was pretty cagey about what she had been up to for the last few years since graduating from college. She alluded to some boring job she had taken overseas but wouldn't elaborate.

"I could tell you more, lover boy," she joked, "but then I'd have to kill you."

Fair enough. I couldn't really reveal too much about my life either, what with my involvement in national defense. And yet, she kept prying. She acted hurt when I wasn't forthcoming.

"You're my man, *Idjmnukolpyumup*. My mate. It doesn't feel right that you're keeping secrets from me."

I shrugged helplessly.

"What do you think I am," she said, "some sort of spy?"

Shadow wore me down. After a while, I guess I started letting things slip out. I have a hard time remembering the exact moments, or the details. She was skilled, tapping me for intel without me even realizing it. Looking back, I've figured out her tactics. She rewarded me with a little kiss every time I gave her a piece of classified info. I was like a trained dog doing tricks for a treat. It's humiliating now to think I could ever have been such a pathetic, love-drunk chump.

I was still blissfully unaware that I was married to a covert enemy agent when I got a summons from my CO back at the base. Being an asset of the special forces, and essentially government property, I had a tracking chip implanted in my neck. Colonel Cramer used it to find me through a military satellite and then sent in a drone-lifted communication device with a secure and direct line to his headquarters.

"I need a squad leader, sergeant. Pronto."

"I'd like to oblige, Don, but I'm kind of on my honeymoon."

"You're going to want in on this one, Charlie."

I sighed. "What do ya got?"

"It's a code seventeen," he said, "but with a complication."

I waited.

A cloudburst had just opened up over the alpine meadow where Shadow and I were camped.

I watched my wife walking away from me naked in the storm.

"It's your brother," said Cramer.

Shadow's brown skin damped with rain.

"Cody's been compromised, Charlie. He's being held prisoner."

# 36

*Lance*

One evening, after a long training session of absorbing blows from Atu's fists and feet, I joined Eo on one of the platforms suspended near the ceiling of the Ark. As the twilight faded, a moonless night materialized beyond the rectangular opening above us. Eo adjusted the telescope on the platform, squinting through the eyepiece with her blue eye. She then stepped back, directing me to look through the viewer myself. I did so, observing a faintly lustrous nebula in the center of the vision field.

"What am I looking at?"

"The light of a distant galaxy. The one toward which the Highborns launched their transport biome."

"Why did they go there?"

"Because of all the corners of the universe, that is the closest one our scientists believed held a planet most with the characteristics of our own before the freeze."

"Are they there now?"

"Perhaps. Unless they are still en route."

It was an almost incomprehensible concept to grasp, even when returning to the nonhuman perspective of my former self as a machine with a limited sense of impermanence. The

Highborn's ship had been traveling through space for a whole eon, a length of time manyfold beyond the entire evolution of the human species.

"When I need reassurance," said Eo "I meditate on that far away corner of the heavens. It is how I connect with my child."

If that planet was anything at all like Earth, it had already gone through many disruptive changes in the span of their journey, possibly even making it uninhabitable for the Highborns by the time they finally arrived. Although it would have been a relevant topic for discussion, I refrained from pointing this out to Eo, as I felt disinclined to undermine her sense of well-being, no matter how ill-conceived it might be.

"You believe your daughter is still alive?"

"I do. She has grown into her adult form since I last held her to my breast, but I have every reason to believe she is enjoying a full and rewarding life." Eo raised a palm toward the sky. "I know she is living, Lance. I can feel her over the distance."

I considered this to be dubious mathematics, but again, I refrained from making comment. In my original design as an amorous companion droid, I had been programmed with an exaggerated capacity for caring and empathy. Although I had learned to override those sentiments through my own force of will, I found this impossible to do with Eo. It occurred to me in that moment that I had inadvertently developed confusing, human-like feelings for her. The last thing I wanted was to hurt my friend, even if I secretly believed she was entertaining a fairytale.

"Someday," said Eo, "my child will return from heaven to earth, and we will be reunited. That is my inspiration, the unreasonable hope by which I live my life."

We stood side-by-side on the platform, both of us gazing through the dark hole overhead.

"I know what you are thinking, Lance."

I shrugged, resisting the temptation to make my thought processes audible.

"You assume I am living by a double standard. On the one hand, I am forever deriding humans for their weakness of relying on childish fictions to get them through their day, while on the other I appear to be living by the unreasonable hope of my own personal religion."

"You are an exceedingly intelligent creature, Eo. I'm sure you know more about the subject than I do."

She softly laughed. "You're a sweetheart, Lance."

For some reason this flustered me. Sweetheart? Although I had a vast catalog of situational responses to draw from, I found myself inexplicably tongue-tied by her endearment.

"It is merely science, Lance. Quantum physics, to be exact."

"Please explain."

"By focusing my life force energy, I am able to link the subatomic particles between myself and my offspring. With this method, I build a bridge through space which allows me to interact with her. It is a tenuous connection, but through it we enjoy a rudimentary form of communication."

This struck me as similar to the questionable practice of prayer to the even more questionable figure of a deity. "But your child must be many million kilometers away."

"The universe is a single object, Lance. All parts are connected to the whole. It is like a body." Eo ran her fingers down my arm. "No matter where I touch your person, your entire body becomes aware of me. Although space is largely nothing but emptiness, it is simultaneously a single continuum of interconnected bits."

I raised my hand before my face, waving it in the seemingly empty air.

"It is from this phenomenon," said Eo, "that humans get their notions of spirits and gods. They sense it at special times. When holding their child. When watching the moon. When having intercourse with their mate. Through these heightened moments, they vaguely feel their own interconnection with all things, but their lives are too brief and distracted for them to fully understand and develop its potential. Instead, they mislay the mystery. They twist it into idolatry. They place the cosmic singularity outside of themselves, losing sight of their role as parts of the whole."

I considered this as a reasonable fact.

"This telephysical skill is essentially maternal," said Eo. "A child is such an integral part of its mother, both of them sharing a relatively closed and intimate system during gestation. It is perhaps too abstract a maneuver for anyone who hasn't undergone the phenomenon of carrying a child to term in their womb."

Being male by design, and motherless, I found myself slightly resentful of her comments. Although I had to allow that they were most likely correct.

"The very Deilonium coursing through my cells allows me a direct link to the process," said Eo. "While current scientific thinking bestows masculine characteristics on that metaphysical element, it is intrinsically female by its nature and is omnipresent throughout the universe.

"Deilonium is not aggressive and seminal," she said, "but nurturing and amniotic.

"It does not spring from the loins of some God the Father, but from Mother Nature's cosmological womb."

# 37

## *Charlie*

And just like that the honeymoon was over.

Colonel Cramer sent in a Flashpoint jet copter to pluck me out of the wilderness. The onboard intel officer briefed me as I traveled to the drop point where I'd meet up with my team.

Understandably, I was distracted. This mission included a personal snag I wasn't used to. Cody's jam was making it hard for me to concentrate and stay objective. Although this wasn't my first rodeo by a longshot, I was struggling with some serious guilt issues this go round. Sure, I'd only been born about five minutes before Cody, but that technically made me his big brother. That role came with certain responsibilities. I should have been there for him when things went tits up. Instead, I was off indulging in matrimonial bliss. He'd never even be in this fix if I'd been doing my job.

And yet, it was more than that.

Something…

I couldn't put my finger on it.

At that point, it was still subconscious, just a niggling in the back of my stupid brain, some dark shape lurking in the gaps between my more lucid thoughts.

Shadow had acted so aloof when we said our goodbyes. She didn't seem a bit surprised when a high-end military aircraft dropped out of the clouds to whisk me away. It was almost as if she'd been expecting it. That alone felt odd. But there was something else…

We had just enjoyed the best summer of our lives, and now, suddenly, we were being thrust into the next phase of our life together. I guess I expected more support from her, at least some sort of acknowledgement of all we'd just been through together, and all we had ahead of us as a married couple. Instead, I was picking up some seriously negative vibes.

"I love you, Shadow."

I said it a little too desperately.

And then I leaned in for a kiss.

Shadow pressed her fingers to my chest and turned away. "I've told you a thousand times," she said. "The name's Diana."

The gesture felt mechanical, as if a switch had been thrown on her emotional control panel.

I didn't have time to work out what it meant right then. My ride was waiting, and some very impatient flyboys were signaling for me to get my ass onboard their whirly bird. But I carried that moment with me.

The way Shadow wouldn't meet my eyes.

The chill in the air around her.

As the chopper lifted away from the ground, I watched my mate hurrying away below, as if she had some pressing appointment to get to, as if she'd already forgotten all about me.

My hands went numb.

Ice settled in my gut.

And then a pair of claws tore into my heart.

# 38

Cody's call sign was R2. Mine was R1. Technically, the R was supposed to stand for Raider, but the joke around Control was that our Rs stood for Redskin.

We didn't mind. We'd grown up with that kind of thing. We knew we were different from the other assets. We knew we were better.

Cody and I had originally been chosen as a two-man squad for the mission in which he'd ultimately been captured – a mission with the code name God Juice. HQ considered it a delicate job requiring the exclusive skill set of the Bear Claw boys. We'd been prepping for two months when I picked up a couple of bullets in my belly while on another assignment. Unfortunately, the orders to execute Operation God Juice came during my downtime back in Wyoming.

Colonel Cramer had to make some quick calculations.

Risks to benefits.

Odds for success.

In the end, he couldn't let the opportunity pass.

He let R2 fly this one solo.

The objective was some crackerjack biochemist who had been pushing the envelope of the possible, conducting diabolical experiments with elements on a subatomic level. He was looking for ways to tap into quantum powers beyond the magnitude of anything yet discovered.

Yeah, I know. Where do these kooks come from?

While doing field work in Indonesia, our mad scientist came across an unknown element at a thermal vent in a volcano crater. He managed to capture and isolate a sample of the stuff and then transport it to his lab. He dubbed his discovery Deilonium, the prefix of the name coming from the Latin word for God.

I guess you could say he had *Dei*lusions of grandeur.

Although he believed Deilonium held supernatural properties, our nutty professor wasn't able to harness its potential. That's what got him into trouble. He began consulting with colleagues around the globe, picking their brains for data that would help him crack his nut. At first, he was guarded with his fellow eggheads, but then his ego got the better of him. He started bragging and blabbing about his find. When he claimed that Deilonium was the end-all-be-all foundational element of the universe, capable of bestowing eternal life in one application while creating cataclysmic destruction in another, someone was listening in.

They nabbed him and his wife and daughter from their beds in the night. Along with his magical element.

Next, they dragged him off to a highly secure lab in an undisclosed corner of a Middle Eastern desert. The outfit who had kidnapped our man wasn't affiliated with the usual coalitions of chaos and anarchy. And it wasn't associated with any particular country either. Control could never completely figure out who it was, although it was always suspected that they had ties to Thorson. This gang was expert at covering their tracks. All we knew was that they were an independent entity and obviously had a shitload of money behind their operation. Even though it sounded like something out of a comic book, our top brass decided they couldn't take any chances on Deilonium being an actual threat. They couldn't allow some rogue organization to use it to take over the world.

It took our people over a month to locate the target.

Once they did, Cody and I started laying the groundwork for infiltration and extraction.

# 39

## *Lance*

In the months since I had first boarded the Ark, I continuously reworked my tactics for fulfilling my objectives. Each time I acquired new information, I refined the weapons in my intellectual arsenal in accordance with the expansion of my knowledge base, incorporating what was pertinent to my ultimate purpose while relegating that which was not. I assimilated the physical skills I learned from Atu. I catalogued the cerebral lessons I learned from books. And, of course, I integrated the philosophical conversations I enjoyed with Eo.

Initially, my goals were well defined.

Using my newly acquired skills, I would hunt down my enemies one by one and destroy them.

But after some months of laying the groundwork for this venture, I found myself becoming less, rather than more, focused on my ambitions. It was as if my ratiocinative capacity had been infected with a destabilizing virus. My certitude wavered. My thought signals became jumbled. And my objectives grew evermore obscure, as if fading behind the fogs drifting over the Skelton Coast.

Finally, I found it necessary to perform an in-depth diagnostic of my thought processes and data assimilation.

Through this procedure, I discovered the surprising fact that my mission drift was being caused by a single factor – my growing fondness for Eo.

This variable was perplexing.

It presented a dilemma.

In one respect, I was dependent upon Eo for the information I needed to fulfill my mission, but in an equal regard, my developing feelings for her were undermining the very aspiration toward which I was striving. The obvious answer to this problem was for me to override my affection for my mentor and actively objectify our relationship. With this intention, I set about reprogramming myself and adopting a fully detached disposition.

In my first attempt, I failed.

I adjusted my calibrations, rebooted my works matrix, and tried again.

Only to fail once more.

It was at that moment that I came to understand a point previously lost to me as a mathematically driven construct – an emotion can have just as much power as a physical force.

This upended my concept of the concrete world in which I had believed myself to be a part and thrust me into a realm of nonmaterial energy systems. It was a revelation that had been staring me in the face ever since I had felt my first suggestions of tenderness for Moxie. But now, alarmingly, I was experiencing that metaphysical process once again, this time while being fully aware of its root cause.

I had fallen in love with Eo.

That was the unequivocal factor in this equation.

As well as the cause for my internal confusion.

Upon formulating this insight, I found myself immediately seized with the conflicting emotions of both guilt and elation.

At one turn, I felt as if I had betrayed my connection to Moxie. After all, she was my ideal, my destiny's ill-fated counterpart, and the angel to whose memory I had pledged my eternal devotion.

And yet, when my thought patterns shifted to Eo, I found my componentry surging with an overpowering happiness.

The musical frequency of her voice.

The acuity of her observations.

The prismatic configuration of her gaze.

And the cumulative, ineffable qualities of her as an intelligent, sentient life form.

The contemplation of these fractional aspects of Eo, when joined into a single whole, overwhelmed me with electrical joy. Meanwhile, my memories of Moxie lurked like guilty shadows between my more exultant thoughts of Eo.

Another epiphany then came to me when I realized that this same variety of confusion was at the core of why one should never trust a human. The species was unreliable by nature of its faulty design. For surely every member of the human race was susceptible to some variant of this pandemic.

Love was the sickness to which no human was immune.

It overpowered their common sense and caused them to act irrationally.

I had heard this theme in their music.

I had read it in their novels and poems.

And now, I realized with dismay, I myself had devolved into a version of that same sentimental matter made so vulnerable by this distressing human defect.

# 40

## *Charlie*

Like me, Cody had a tracking chip in his neck, but for Operation God Juice, he had also been fitted with a backup chip in his ankle. Cramer didn't want to take any chances on losing him. This proved a good move by the colonel. Cody's captors found and destroyed the first chip, but they overlooked chip number two. That's how our comms team was able to locate Cody and the biochemist. They picked up a single, very faint blip from his distress beacon. By tracking his signal, they determined that both prisoners had been relocated to a remote island in the Indian Ocean.

As far as tropical islands go, this one wasn't much to look at. Just a jagged little mountain of volcanic rock poking up from a stretch of empty ocean. The only sign of life on the island was a rookery of nesting sea birds.

Our satellites gathered zero intel at first go, so aerial recon tried contouring the landmass with seismic imaging equipment. All they came up with was an impenetrable core. No radiation. No sounds or radio transmissions. All of which seemed unlikely for a volcanic protrusion being used as a high-end laboratory in the business of dissecting molecules, so they monitored the island 24-7 with atmospheric drones until… Bingo! They caught something on radar.

There were several underwater openings around the island's perimeter, indicating that it was interwoven with empty lava tubes, all most likely leading to a sizeable interior chamber. When a peculiar shadow passed into one of the larger openings, they snapped photos for analysis. That's when they figured out that the whole compound was being serviced by stealth subs of a design undetectable by sonar.

Now we had a better idea of what we were up against.

These baddies were super high-tech and super cautious.

Time to initiate God Juice, phase 2.

———

There were six of us on the extraction team. Two women and four men. Usually we were one more, but our number seven – Cody – was currently indisposed. We called ourselves Easy Company as an homage to our favorite comic book heroes in *Sgt. Rock*. I had worked with these commandos on exactly nineteen other missions. They were a gung-ho bunch of jarheads, highly skilled and highly reliable – the most capable squad on the planet.

We couldn't just drop straight in on our target without being discovered, so we were snuck onto a container ship traveling the nearest sea lane. Once we were at the closest point to the island, we launched our own submersible – a claustrophobic little pod powered by compressed air that traveled at a depth of just twenty fathoms. No moving metal parts or engine noise. Virtually undetectable. Just a directional stream of bubbles propelling us along like a giant grouper with a bad case of the farts.

At four klicks out, we disembarked from the submersible, pulled its plugs, and sent it to the bottom of the ocean. The sub was disposable, made entirely of a leave-no-trace organic material that was designed to begin biodegrading within twenty-four hours, ultimately becoming nothing but a disintegrating mass of plant proteins and starches dissolving into the saltwater. Cramer didn't want us leaving any signs that we were ever there. He was cautious that way.

From there, we continued on with canned air and swim fins. We wore thermal cloak wetsuits to get us past any heat sensors. As long as we stayed underwater, we would also be hidden from their motion detectors, or possibly only be mistaken for a family of frolicking dugongs. Once we surfaced…well, then we'd have to improvise.

We didn't know what kind of resistance we'd meet once inside. What sort of sec units did they employ? And how heavily were they armed? We were hoping it would be easy pickings, but the compound's bunker design had made it impossible to gather enough intel for us to know for sure.

Our recon people identified a murky cloud of sediment escaping from one of the smaller lava tubes at the base of a cliff, indicating, according to their readings, a passage to the inner cavity of the island. That was our first objective.

The door to the funhouse.

# 41

*Lance*

Although there would always be more portals for me to open into the fathomless depths of knowledge, I had reached a pivotal point in my education. My databank of the human behavioral sciences, while arguably incomplete in all of its aggregations, had finally expanded enough for me to embark on my campaign of vengeance.

My confidence was further reinforced during one of my lessons with Atu. We had been training in our usual manner, but with different results. For the first time, I was able to avoid his blows while landing many of my own. It seemed I had finally learned to redirect my opponent's aggressive energy back to its source.

How had I achieved this?

What had changed?

It occurred to me that my new abilities were an inadvertent side effect of my feelings for Eo. Upon admitting to myself that I cared for her, I had permitted my amorous thoughts to move to the fore of my attention zone, while simultaneously relegating all other issues to the depths of my structured gel brain. In doing so, I had allowed a detachment to take over in my physical actions. I had temporarily forgotten about the hunter, Thorson, and even Moxie. I had forgotten about my vendetta and my rage. This allowed me to fight with the objectivity Atu had been advocating. At the same time, the exhilaration caused by my thoughts of Eo had filled me with an indomitable strength. In a very quantifiable way, I was now being powered by Love.

At the end of our training session, Atu regarded me curiously and did something he had never done before. He shook my hand. Next, while gazing directly into my eyes, he nodded, emitting a positively inflected grunt.

Such, I realized, was what passed for a graduation speech from my taciturn instructor.

Eo had been watching us quietly from the shadows and stepped across the room.

"Thank you, Atu," she said. "You have taught him well."

Atu bowed to us both and summarily left the Ark, traveling inland over the sunlit dunes.

Eo smiled and laced her fingers in mine. "Come with me, Lance."

A pleasing sensation buzzed through my pleasure sensors as we strolled hand in hand through the Ark.

———————

A relaxed familiarity settled between us as Eo led me through the less frequented byways of her home.

We moved without speaking through the dark narrow passageways accessing the ship's larger interior compartments. Our footfalls echoed against the tomb-like silence in the maze of iron-hewn caverns.

Eventually, we came to the engine room, with its row upon row of defunct instruments. Cracked gauges, broken levers, and rusted valves. A twisted network of pipes disappeared into the ceiling. Someone – perhaps one of the original sailors – had painted graffiti across the walls. The images were reminiscent of primitive cave paintings, their meanings known only to the artist, lost long ago to the forgetfulness of time.

I had read many novels in the past months, and many poems. Through their study, I had developed the human aptitude for seeing things metaphorically. It seemed to me that this walk through the Ark was somehow meant to be symbolic. Eo was taking me on a meaningful tour.

But of what?

In some respects, I could not help but note the similarities between the Ark and myself. Although we had been manufactured for different purposes, we were both machines. We had both been made by men to serve mankind. Or, in my case, womankind – specifically, my owner Judy Baxter. Since running aground, the Ark had become one of the many derelict ruins littering the Skeleton Coast. On its surface, it appeared to be nothing more than an oxidizing titan in a graveyard of dead machines. Was this fate awaiting us all in one form or another? And was this tour of the Ark Eo's oblique suggestion to make much of time? Or was that simply my own newly configured symbol-making facility interpreting the moment to meet my own expanding desires?

*Gather ye Rose-buds while ye may,* read the poem that came to my mind.

And yet, in another respect, I saw our tour as a privileged access into the private workings of Eo herself. She had repurposed this nautical ruin just as she had repurposed me.

She had given us both a second chance, a rebirth. This ship was the manifestation of her maternal ability to give new life to something that had seemed irrevocably inanimate. In like manner, she had become my own resurrector, my personal Deilonium-infused savior.

After visiting the ship's fantail, we climbed a flight of steps into the main chamber. The afternoon had slipped into the evening, filling the room with a close velvet darkness. The scientific apparatuses loomed overhead on their platforms like beasts dozing in their nests.

We moved among the paintings and tapestries and towering bookshelves, filled as they were with all of their distillations of human thoughts and emotions. As we passed, it seemed as if their contents were downloading into our souls. All of their poignant invocations of humanity. All of their absurdities and contradictions, along with their accompanying sorrows and joys.

We walked past the foot of the holographic tree, its semitransparent branches drooping with fruit like bytes of knowledge to be plucked and consumed and assimilated.

*The line between opposites is thin* was the insight that mysteriously registered with me in that moment.

Rage and peace – divinity and science – ignorance and knowledge – life and death.

Even fighting and making love.

"Here we are," said Eo.

And then she kissed me.

We had arrived at her enormous bed – a microcosm of pillows and twisted blankets.

A black hole, a galaxy, a womb.

The bed's gravity tugged at us.

And yet, something in me resisted. I realized then that this entire tour of the Ark had served as a prelude to this moment of truth, a kind of foreplay to our graduated relationship and its inevitable intimacy.

Eo squeezed my fingers. "Why so shy, Lance? I understood you to be made for this?"

Upon quickly evaluating my hesitation, I found that I was reluctant to let go of my former motivations. Something in the impending act would negate all that I had worked so hard to achieve. Likewise, it would downgrade my sacred memories of Moxie.

"It's just…" I formulated an excuse. "I've never made love with a billion-year-old female before."

Eo laughed. "Well," she said, "if it makes you feel any better, in my whole long life I have never once made love with a two-year-old intellectualized mechanoid."

Somehow that reassured me.

Indicating that the love virus had infected my intellect.

And so, helpless to do otherwise, I took her in my arms.

# 42

## *Charlie*

My team penetrated the compound by way of an ancient lava tube.

I led the way.

We squirmed through the opening like flagellating gametes working into the uterine depths of the island.

Sure, it was a weird time to be using reproductive sex metaphors, but those kinds of thoughts always came to me whenever I entered caves or bear dens.

Freud again.

That rat bastard.

Over the course of my military career, I had learned that carefully planned missions almost always reveal weaknesses in the enemy's line of defense. At first blush, this one appeared to be no exception. As cautious as our adversaries were, they hadn't protected against our chosen entry. Apparently, their security people had decided only suicidal idiots would be stupid enough to try breaching the compound by this particular route. It didn't take long before I started thinking maybe they were right.

It was tight.

And fallopian dark.

Our masks were equipped with night vision lenses, lending a ghoulish green eeriness to the experience. At several points we had to remove our tanks and feed them and our larger weapons through the hole ahead of us. Although it was time consuming, this was working fine until my second – Fitch – got trapped in a constriction. After some spine-popping yoga moves, I was able to turn around and get ahold of his harness straps and pull.

But no good.

He didn't budge.

Things were further complicated by the fact that we were proceeding under radio silence. We didn't dare risk having the hostiles picking up on our signal. That meant I had no idea what was happening on the other side of this human plug. Were they pulling or pushing or what?

To his credit, Fitch remained calm.

Unfortunately, he also remained stuck.

Time was slipping away.

As was our precisely calculated air supply.

Being squad leader meant that I was in the hotseat for making some fast, appropriate decisions. And yet, no matter how I worked the math, I could only come up with one sorry ass answer to this problem – I was going to have to leave Fitch to die a slow and terrible death. The others would have to decide what to do for themselves. It wasn't in our code of honor to abandon a fellow warrior, but the hopelessness of the situation might undermine that noble practice this time around. The rest of my team would either drown trying to save Fitch, or they would use their dwindling oxygen reserves to get back out the way we came in. I was betting on option number two since there was still a chance for the mission to meet with some level of success.

A slim chance, but a chance.

My guess was that they would hide out for a while under the sea cliffs to give me time to execute some variation of our original plan before they either engaged in the conflict themselves or called in the jet copters to get us out.

Fitch knew what I was thinking. It was written all over his eerie green face.

He looked at me for a long moment through his mask, letting it all sink in. We all knew what we'd signed up for. The risks. Dying was always a strong possibility.

Finally, Fitch nodded once, accepting his fate.

You had to give the man some serious respect.

I felt like an A-number-one rat fink but saw no other choice if I was going to get my brother back.

After giving Fitch a solemn salute, I twisted back around in the tube and continued on alone.

# 43

After a few more turns, the tube widened into a little room where I could get my head out of the water. I checked the gauge on my air tank – empty.

No big deal. I was tired of dealing with the damn thing anyway.

I ditched my tank and fins. I also dropped my chop rifle. The bigger weapon was cumbersome and would only be useful in a full-blown shootout. Without my team to back me up, that was something I was hoping to avoid. I kept my standard issue pistol for disabling humans, and my handheld burst ray for toasting robots. And of course, my trusty hunting knife stayed strapped to my lower leg.

I breathed up.

And then I continued on in freediving mode, hoping like heck that I wouldn't run into a dead end, or some hungry sea monster with a craving for Native American sushi.

In the past, my grandfather's voice would come to me at times like these. He'd offer me some mumbo-jumbo advice about becoming one with the water or turning myself into a man-trout. And yet, the old man was strangely silent at the moment. I don't know. I was too busy to sort it out right then, but I kind of got the feeling he was mad at me.

Wiggling on through the tube, I pulled myself along over the slimy rocks, until I saw a glimmer ahead and kicked toward it.

It was a struggle to keep from coughing and wheezing and otherwise making a racket when I broke the surface. My lungs were about to bust, and my skull felt like it was going to split. Sucking air, I stroked into the shadows. Then I lifted my mask and surveyed the scene.

The pool opened into a broad interior bay with a state-of-the-art infrastructure. Lots of stainless-steel girders, a concrete pier, cargo cranes, and bright lights. A trio of large entryways led into the stone walls, accessing the subterranean depths of the facility.

Two large submarines were moored at the dock. They weren't of your standard militaristic make. The engineers must have been smoking reefer when they designed these retro-futuristic beauties. They looked like the resultant spawn of a humpback whale fornicating with a 1960s Oldsmobile.

About twenty personnel of various ethnicities were moving around and performing different tasks. The clandestine organization who hired them obviously gathered its talent from all over the world. That would help me out since I was off-color myself. There were no logos on their uniforms indicating any kind of an organization or affiliation with a country. The few words I could see on signs and doorways were all in English, so I presumed that was the lingua franca of the place. Many of the crew wore weapons on their hips, with a few of them carrying stubby brip rifles slung over their shoulders.

Surveillance cameras were posted at different points around the cavern. The system appeared to be extensive, with no gaps in visual coverage. I expected as much, but it was still disappointing. It looked like I'd have to become invisible. Luckily, that was one of the tricks in my repertoire.

A wide platform ran along the wall on the far side of the bay. It was stacked with crates next to a desalination pump. A network of pipes ran out of the pump in all directions like the arms of a giant octopus. A technician was servicing the intake filters. The procedure required him to climb down through a manhole in the platform where it joined the dock. He'd disappear for a minute, work down in the hole, and then come back up to grab another tool or piece of equipment from his work cart. He wore a wetsuit and a dive mask, indicating that he was working in the water.

That looked like my in. I slid my mask back into place and pulled a few deep breaths before I dove and crossed the bay and swam under the dock.

I rose up out of the depths and dragged him into the water.

The whole struggle lasted less than a minute.

After hiding my weapons in his tool bag, I crawled out of the manhole and scanned the scene while casually rummaging through the pipes and couplers in the back of the electric cart. Next, I climbed into the front seat with the tool bag beside me. The workman's passkey was hanging by a lanyard on the start button. I hung it around my neck.

The primary objective of Operation God Juice was to seize and secure the biochemist along with his wife and daughter and his jar of hocus-pocus. Only after that priority was accomplished were we allowed to try for Cody, and only if it didn't otherwise compromise the mission. Colonel Cramer had made that clear at our team briefing. But I didn't see it that way. For one thing, I wasn't convinced that this chemist was anything more than a crackpot who'd just made himself important by telling a big lie. Deilonium sounded a little too much like sci-fi crapola to me. By my way of looking at it, my brother's life was what mattered, not some phony and his pipe dream.

Priority one for R1 was to rescue R2.

I unzipped the pocket on my wetsuit and reached in for the tracking device synced to the beacon in Cody's ankle. I flipped the switch, got a bearing on his location, and switched it off. The whole process took less than two seconds, not enough time for their monitors to register anything more than an insignificant burp in their system.

After that, I drove the cart along the platform, turning through the second entryway leading into the guts of the compound. I nodded and waved to the other folks along the way, passing myself off as just another member of their crew.

Hang on, Cody. The posse's on its way.

# 44

## *Lance*

Intercourse with someone you love is an entirely more pleasing experience than obligatorily performing the procedure for your owner!

This fact registered with me at exactly one minute and eight seconds into the act.

Amorous interaction with Eo was not the motor-driven program I had always initiated and fulfilled for Judy Baxter, but a transcendent improvisation powered by the spontaneity of genuine fondness.

It was the magical quality encrypted in poetry.

It was the ineffable miracle embedded within the aurora borealis.

It was so much more than I can say.

And yet, the very inadequacy of my lexical index to provide words for its expression made the experience seem all the more unquantifiable and infinite. For the first time since my manufacture, I realized what Eo had referred to as the singularity of the cosmos. Joining with her was an intimate reenactment of the Big Bang.

Her kisses were quantum explosions.

Her pleasurable moans the echoes of eternity.

---

Afterwards, Eo and I lay close with one another and watched the moon, round and luminous, drifting slowly across the rectangular opening in the ceiling of the Ark.

No speech was necessary between us right then, and yet a specific word eventually came to me all the same.

It traveled over the light years from the deepest regions of the universe.

It floated down with the photons of moonlight.

Until it settled in my thought signals like the title of a prehistoric lullaby.

The word's subtle power welled inside of me, seeking utterance, and so I offered it back to the night.

*"Katoyotapsommiki,"* I whispered. *"Katoyotapsommiki."*

# 45

## *Charlie*

I drove as far as I could into the complex and parked the cart at a charging station, plugging a cord into the vehicle's port to make it look official. Next, I proceeded on foot, carrying the tool bag with my weapons in one hand and a length of steel pipe in the other. I came to a sliding glass door with a security check system that included a thumbprint scanning device. A pair of women was coming through from the other side.

"Could you hold that please?"

I lifted my burdens to show that my hands were full and gestured with my chin to the passkey hanging around my neck to assure them that I was authorized and in the database. They didn't ask any questions and held the door – no doubt a violation of their security protocol. My charming, primitive smile had obviously disarmed them.

"Thanks."

I braced myself in case the scanner didn't like my guns, but the door slid closed behind me without any sirens going off.

Although I was pulling off a pretty good act as a mild-mannered handyman, I was beginning to feel conspicuous.

The wetsuit's what did it. When I came to a maintenance supply room, I stepped inside and locked the door behind me. After checking for cameras, I peeled off my wet togs and put on one of the jumpsuits hanging in the closet. I also snagged a pair of sneakers and a ball cap.

Once I'd taken another quick reading with my tracker, I reentered the corridor, still carrying the bag and pipe.

Cody was close now.

Just another thirty meters into the maze.

A man passed me in the hallway. And a woman. Then I came around a corner to find a pair of armed guards standing on either side of a door.

This had to be it.

———

Sometimes God is just another word for good timing.

When a believer tells you about some miracle in their life, chances are they're referring to nothing but a fluky convergence of circumstances. Of course, a godless psychologist might call the same thing synchronicity or blame it on the mysterious workings of the collective unconscious. Either way, it's easy to see how a desperate sap might interpret such a coincidence as divine intervention.

I walked down the hallway in front of the guards, humming a tune.

"Hey, boys. How's it hangin'?"

In response, they both adjusted their grip on their brip guns, their trigger fingers poised and twitching.

Oh, great, I thought. Competent jailers.

There was a service panel in the wall directly across from them. I nodded toward it and said, "Time to do a little repair work on the air circulator."

They gave me a dirty look but didn't speak.

I shrugged and stepped over to the panel. Kneeling on the floor, I unzipped my bag. After calculating the angle and ballistics, I decided the occasion called for two quick head shots. I watched my targets in my peripheral vision. They were following my every move. If I missed a beat, I'd be bripped apart.

Quick and accurate, I told myself. You miss, you die.

I reached into my bag and pulled out a screwdriver and laid it on the floor. Then I pulled out a socket wrench. Taking a breath, I reached in one more time, wrapped my hand around my pistol, and then…

An alarm went off.

Both guards drew down on me.

"Hands up!"

Damn!

I let go of the gun and raised my hands.

"Hands behind your head!"

"Fellas, I'm just…"

"Do it!"

What choice did I have?

Alarms blared throughout the compound. I figured someone had found the guy I'd bumped off in the manhole. Or maybe my team had broken their radio silence and enemy surveillance had picked up on their chatter. Whatever the case, I was basically cooked.

That's when the agent of God – aka Mr. Timely Coincidence – piped up over the intercom.

"Attention! All security personnel are to report to the bay

area immediately. Defcon One! I repeat, Defcon One!"

The message was repeated two more times. Panic tremored the announcer's voice while gunfire popped in the background.

The two guards forgot all about me and headed down the hall at a full gallop.

I grabbed my weapons out of the bag and went to the door. It was locked, so I shot the latch and kicked it in.

A man was lying on a cot on the far side of the narrow room, face to the wall.

"Hey!" I yelled.

My stomach dropped when the guy rolled over and sat up. He looked like he'd been in a fight with a bulldozer. Bruised and bashed. And kind of bent to one side.

Still, I couldn't help but grin. "Hiya, little brother. Guess who's here."

Cody coughed and nodded and held his ribs.

———————

We didn't have time for a brotherly reunion of happy hugs and kisses.

Instead, I knelt before Cody and held his shoulders. His face was purple and swollen. He gazed wearily into my eyes and asked, "What took you so long?"

"Sorry about that. You good to go?"

"You bet," he said, *"Anyo lo watsneesu!"* which was a phrase we used as kids, basically the Chompquaw equivalent for Let's blow this pop stand!

I grinned again and gave him my pistol, keeping the burst ray and knife for myself.

The commotion in the bay had to be coming from my team. Somehow, they'd infiltrated the compound and now they were wreaking some serious havoc. With Cody in such a bad way, it didn't make sense to throw him into the fight. Operation God Juice had officially gone hard sideways. Time to abort.

The voice crackled over the intercom with a new announcement. "Evac code 3R7 has been initiated. All personnel are to proceed accordingly."

Next, we found ourselves in a stampede of lab-coated science nerds, all of them scared shitless and heading toward the submarine bay.

I turned to Cody. "Is there another way out?"

"Follow me."

Limping, he led me down a side hall to a ladder disappearing into the ceiling. I peered up the ladder to where it ended at a hatch about sixty feet above us.

"Can you do it?" I asked.

After tucking the pistol into his waistband, he bobbed his head. "I'm right behind you."

Cody struggled after me, his breathing ragged. Every few feet, he'd stop to rest, hooking his arms in the metal rungs and coughing painfully in the dead air of the shaft. I swear I could hear his broken bones grinding.

"You've got this, little brother. I'll go on up and work the door."

"Copy that," he gasped.

The hatch was pressure sealed. When I twisted the latch, air whooshed up the shaft and hissed around the edges of the door, jerking it out of my hands and popping the lid to a blinding wash of sunlight.

We crawled out onto a rocky slope.

It was surprisingly peaceful.

A pair of gulls drifted lazily over our heads.

The sea sparkled in all directions.

You'd never have known there was a life-or-death battle going on.

Until… *Thum-whomp! Thum-whomp!*

Small caliber Torb concussion canons.

Which meant remotely operated dronebots.

Chop rifles answered the Torbs, and then Easy Company came over the rise, alternating between running and returning fire. I counted all five of our people. Everyone had made it.

Including Fitch!

I waved my arms and yelled them over.

Although Command had eyes in the sky and was watching the whole hot mess, I put in a distress call to hurry them along.

"R1 to Angel Mother. Mayday! Mayday! Lock in our position at two-niner Bravo west Zulu! We need air fire and team extraction now!"

With any luck, the cavalry would arrive within a couple minutes.

Of course, a lot can happen in a minute.

# 46

## *Lance*

On the day after I made love with Eo, I walked one half kilometer north of the Ark and sat on a high dune. My intention was to put some distance between myself and my significant other in order to more clearly evaluate my ambitions in light of recent events and my accelerated knowledge acquisition.

A pair of gulls soared aerodynamically over my head.

While the sea kaleidoscopically refracted the sun's rays before me.

To my right lay a whale's skeleton, its bleached bones spread out like a diagram in a biology textbook.

Death reveals a clinical beauty, I realized, upon studying the mammal's remains. An indifferent equilibrium. This primitive creature, once wandering the oceans just as a starship might wander through outer space, was now reduced to its fundamental armature – the very framework upon which its life-infused flesh had once hung. A flesh encoded with personal experiences. A little world of secrets and dreams. All cumulatively packaged in its cells from the orgasmic spasm of its genesis all the way to the apocalyptic implosion of its final breath.

The marvels it must have seen in the interim.

And still, I wondered if this leviathan could ever have imagined the day when a sapient, synthetic man would be admiring its naked bones on the shores of the Land God Made in Anger.

———————

I had recently read *Frankenstein* and found the parallels between myself and the monster in that novel to be alarming. In no way did I want my fate to correspond with the tragic fate of that miserable creature. Having no one to love, or to love him in return, that manmade beast had turned to rage and its affiliate deeds of revenge and murder, all leading to catastrophic consequences for everyone involved.

Murder and revenge, I realized, were the very acts I had been contemplating myself.

Having Moxie taken away from me had given birth to the monster of my own rage. But now I was beginning to see that this same rage was only making me grotesque and leading me into unnecessary folly. Why sacrifice the happiness I had found with Eo? Surely, I now had what every man most longs for. And yet, after working so hard and deliberately toward my goal of vengeance, it was difficult to simply let it go.

I had brought a portable computer pad with me to the dune and opened it up on my knees. While doing research for my vendetta during these past months, I had discovered a site on the dark web that served hired killers. The man who had so violently decommissioned Moxie – my nemesis – was listed there as a prime target. He was no longer the hunter but the prey. Although the details of his crime were vague, it was obvious by the unreasonably large price offered for his capture and/or termination that he had greatly angered someone in a position of wealth and power. There were no personal details on the fugitive, only the coordinates of where he had last been seen at a missionary compound in the Congolese jungle. He was listed as "highly dangerous." There was also a photograph.

I knew the face in that photo.

I knew that smug and predatory grin.

The hunter's face had burned onto my hard drive during our previous confrontation in the stratosphere.

Although I hated that man more than any I had ever encountered, I now found the intensity of that emotion to be muted. My love for Eo overpowered it, downgrading that once intense hatred to a barely registered revulsion. The hunter no longer seemed worth the trouble I was devoting to his liquidation.

I sighed like a human and regarded the dead whale beside me.

Then I looked into the hot blue sky.

Something metallic glinted in the sunlight.

I presumed it was a jetliner.

In the next instant, I made my decision – I would abort my mission of revenge!

Instead, I would live forever with Eo. We would enjoy our own personal paradise on the Skeleton Coast. We would be an updated version of Adam and Eve, inhabiting our peaceful garden of books and music and art and love. We would walk the moonlit dunes and watch the sky like devout pilgrims as we waited for the return of Eo's daughter.

Upon articulating this plan, a tension released inside of

me. Had I been made of flesh and blood I would have said that a fever had finally broken after a long illness. I suddenly felt healthy and vibrant, powered by positivity rather than its dark alternative. In short, I was thrilled to be alive.

Although it was an irrational impulse, I experienced an anthropoidal gratitude for the blessings the universe had bestowed upon me and felt moved to thank some supernal force or benevolent god.

Once again, I turned my gaze to the faceless heavens.

"Thank you," I said, and could not help but smile. "Thank you! Thank you! Thank you!"

As if in answer to my words, another metallic glint blinked in the firmament.

And then, in an adjacent sector, another.

My computer simultaneously beeped, drawing my attention. My smile faded as I comprehended the information on the screen.

Two new photographs appeared on the bounty hunter website. One was of the Ark as viewed from high overhead. The other was from the same viewpoint, only zoomed in close on a figure.

This figure, I realized, was myself on the top deck, reading a book.

Probably *Frankenstein*.

The Ark's geographic coordinates were superimposed on the screen over the image, along with a flashing sequence of words –

*Target Sighted – Prepare to Terminate*

# 47

*Charlie*

Eight dronebots stalked over the hill like something out of a monster movie.

My team managed to flank the lead unit and make a kill.

After a volley of well-placed shots, the bot toppled like a lightning-struck Jackpine.

Fitch and the others pulled back to me and Cody, diving behind the embankment just as the bots cut loose with another barrage. The air detonated with Torb beams of directional energy, but the rocks protected us and absorbed the concussion. We laid down return rounds as the bots crept slowly forward in assault formation.

I searched the sky. Where the hell was our air support? Right then, vapor trails appeared out of the blue as our rocket operators dialed their vectors onto the charging dronebots and launched.

"Incoming! Take cover!"

No sooner had I barked the warning than the rockets broke apart high overhead.

"Hell's bells!"

The island was protected from above by a forcefield!

Rocket debris rained down. Incredibly, a chunk conked

one of the bots, knocking it out of commission, but then a nosecone plunged into our own ranks as well. It came down like a flaming hammer, driving right through our sniper. She died instantly.

Suddenly, this was getting real.

Without help from above, we had no choice. We had to take the fight to the bots.

I crawled over to our dead teammate, grabbed her rifle, and tossed it to Cody. He checked the magazine and then gave me the high sign.

"Maneuver time!" I shouted to the others. "Scatter and go!"

It was a risky tactic with so many bots left to take down, but outside of a fatal retreat with our backs to the sea, it was the only option. We needed to buy some time while our evacuation team figured out how to work past the forcefield. We proceeded in pairs, with one commando playing decoy while the other looped around for a shot from behind. If anyone missed a beat, the decoy was dead.

Phase one went well.

Each duo smoked a bot.

The machines lay face down on the battleground, twitching and spewing hydraulic fluid.

Five down, three to go.

Things were looking up.

Just before everything went to hell.

Fitch's partner tripped. In the instant it took for him to get back on his feet, he took a Torb round. He crumpled as the impact turned his guts to gumbo.

Fitch managed to make the shot anyway, but it only disabled the bot's forward mobility. Although the unit was now stationary, it was still in good position for directing its fire at our offensive.

After signaling to Cody, I headed for the wounded bot, coming in from the rear. Its motion detectors picked me up and its turret rotated my way just as I dove to the ground between its legs. The bot's operator didn't dare fire a Torb so close to the unit, so he trained its smaller guns on me. I let loose with a volley from my burst ray, but the angle was wrong and the rays only glanced off the thing's armor. The bot opened fire. I rolled as the bullets tore into the dirt, one of them clipping me in the side. Then I scrambled back through the bot's legs. It swung after me for another shot.

I fell and twisted onto my back, gazing up as the metallic monster lined me up in its sights.

Crap! I thought. I'm toast.

In the next instant, the bot's head dropped onto its chest with an eruption of sparks.

I backflipped out of the way as the monster collapsed. Then I craned around to see who'd made the shot.

My eyes fell on Fitch.

Yeah, that's right. The very guy I'd left for dead had just saved my life.

I gave him a quick high sign.

He was returning the gesture when a Torb round blew him apart.

---

We'd lost another soldier in the chaos. I didn't see how it happened.

Then Cody and our remaining Raider managed to take out

another bot before she was sheared in half by flying shrapnel.

That only left Team Chompquaw.

And one last dronebot.

A final showdown between robots and Indians.

Cody was hurting pretty bad. I could tell by how he was moving. Plus, he was down to his last few bullets. But it didn't really matter. We both knew the situation. We needed to buck up and finish this if we were ever getting off this island alive.

Blood was leaking from my side, but the slug had missed my vitals. My main problem was that my burst ray was out of juice. I scanned the field for another weapon but couldn't find one. That only left one option.

I yanked my grandfather's knife from its scabbard.

The bot must have been running low on ammo too since it had quit throwing out haphazard rounds. The operator was waiting for a good shot. I gave Cody the signal and then we worked our maneuver.

Cody spaced his rifle and pistol shots at calculated intervals, holding the operator's attention while I snuck in from the side. When I was close, I sprinted toward the bot, launching off a boulder with a war whoop and landing on the thing's shoulder. The unit writhed like an enraged grizzly, trying to shake me off. I wrapped my legs and clutched the neck cowling in one hand while stabbing my knife into the eyepiece. The blade glanced off the glass, but I kept pounding until it cracked. The bot kept bucking, but now I had him. My blade gouged the unit's optical intake, shattering the lens.

Somewhere, an operator was now helplessly clutching the joystick of a blind dronebot. He fired off the last of his Torbs and bullets in random directions but didn't hit anything. When his guns started clicking on empty chambers, I dropped to the ground, tucked my knife back in its scabbard, and ran to Cody.

The bot stumbled slowly forward like a man looking for a door in a very dark room.

———

During the fight, our satellites had neutralized the island's forcefield with anion bombardment. Our choppers were now clear for extraction.

Cody and I lay waiting amidst the carnage. Pieces of droncbots and our fellow Raiders littered the battlefield.

It was a sad moment. We'd lost some good friends. Heroes, every one of 'em. But I was happy too. In a weird and guilty sort of way. I'd gotten my brother back.

"There's something I need to tell you, Charlie."

I pressed my palm into my wound and laughed. "Right now?"

"Yeah. You need to know."

"We're almost home, brother. You can tell me later."

"No, Charlie. You need to know." He looked at me hard and cut straight to the point. "Shadow's a spy. She's been using me and you to get intel. She works for the bunch on this island."

"Bullshit!"

But I knew it was true when I heard it. All of the pieces — all of those suspicions that had been lurking in the shadows of my brain — leapt forward into one big vicious, snarling truth.

Cody hung his head. "I'm sorry, Charlie."

My mind flashed to the three of us as kids playing Easy Company. The way we used to hunt and wrestle and read comic books. And then Shadow's words echoed back over the years —

*I'm not dying here in this Indian zoo*, she vowed. *I'm breaking out, boys, no matter what I have to do.*

Her speech had inspired us at the time, but now it sounded like the ultimate voice of doom.

An ice-cold fever flushed through my body.

I felt like I'd taken a Torb round to the soul.

"I should've told you a long time ago, Charlie. How it went down between me and Shadow." Cody shook his head. "I was just too ashamed. I felt like I'd double-crossed you."

I couldn't speak.

"Shadow and me got real close while you were back at Windy Scrub. In that first month after you got hurt. Real close. But something about it felt wrong." Cody's eyes shined wet. "I couldn't do it, Charlie." He looked away. "When I wouldn't marry her, she went to you."

It was a lot to sort out.

A lot to process.

I was suddenly just so damn tired.

But no rest for the wicked.

Now we had a new problem.

I could hear them coming.

Three hover bikes up from the shoreline.

Each one carrying a Masked Slayer.

# 48

*Lance*

The computer toppled from my knees as I stood.

It lay on the sand between my feet, frantically beeping.

By adjusting the focal length of my optics, I was able to zoom in on the objects overhead. Three silver discs hovered at uniform altitudes and equidistant points in the sky. Each had a large black Z painted onto its underside.

I dropped my gaze to the Ark. Eo was standing at the railing, looking my direction from the top deck while shielding her eyes from the sun with a hand. It was a beautiful image. Poetic. Mythical. One I knew I would carry with me always. But it was also melancholic. Even over the distance, I noted the resignation in Eo's posture. The acceptance of her fate.

She lifted her face and opened her arms to the sky.

"Please no," I said.

The briefest of prayers.

In answer, each of the three discs fired a laser beam of particulated antimatter.

The triangulated rays converged on the marooned freighter.

Next, in the space of three tenths of a second, the Ark, my love interest, and all of my newfound hopes for the future, were blown to smithereens.

# 49

*Charlie*

Our choppers were still only specks over the horizon.

The hostiles would get to us first.

I tapped Cody's arm and pointed to the hover bikes heading our way.

Masked Slayers are for-hire assassins dressed like cat burglars – black from head to toe. They don't use weapons. Instead, they snuff their victims with a mix of choke holds and jujitsu. Battlefields aren't their typical venue, but the masterminds behind this organization must have felt they were the best last option after we eliminated their robotic sec units. Cody and I had seen the inside of their operation and now these kickass ninjas had been sent to make sure we didn't get away with any of their secrets.

We were out of ammo, but so what? Bareknuckle brawling was our specialty.

For the moment, all of our issues with Shadow had to be put aside.

"You ready for this, Kemosabe?"

Cody shot me the same grin he always wore as a kid. "You bet, Sarge. Initiate Operation Crazy Redskin."

We crouched back-to-back as the Slayers circled us like

cowboys on horseback. Once they realized we weren't armed, they dismounted and attacked.

Slayer number one went down hard as Cody hooked his ankles.

I pounced and ripped out his throat.

After that, it was one on one.

My guy came at me with rapid-fire jabs, trying to knock me off balance. I let him believe his tactic was working, holding my hands over my face like a sissy, and then falling onto my back. When he lunged, I rammed my heels into his chest and catapulted him on over.

He sprawled in the rocks.

As I jumped onto his back, he swung an elbow - *Crack!* - breaking my nose.

The blow stunned me, giving him time to punch me in the side of the head. My vision went blurry. Blood poured over my mouth. That old taste of trouble. All I could hear was the ocean.

Its motherly voice.

But then, getting louder – the *wup wup wup* of chopper blades slicing the air.

That snapped me out of it and I lurched sideways just as the Slayer sent a skull-crushing boot heel toward my forehead. I grabbed his ankle, heaving upward and cartwheeling him into the dirt. Before he could regroup, I finished him off with a rock.

Then I spun around to find Cody.

My gut flopped when I saw him.

He was on his knees with a Slayer bent behind him, one hand holding his chin, with the other on top of his head.

Cody looked straight into my eyes.

Apologetic. Boyish. Confused. And doomed.

"No," I prayed.

But no good.

With a quick twist, the Slayer snapped his neck.

Cody's lifeless body slumped to the ground.

———

The details get fuzzy after that. All I remember is that I threw everything I had left at that masked angel of death. It's not a smart way to fight if you want to win. Blind rage never works. But I couldn't help myself. I was being driven by uncaged emotion. Despair. Self-loathing. And guilt. All supercharged by Shadow's betrayal.

I absorbed blow after blow but just kept attacking. I was an enraged and wounded animal with nothing left to lose.

Finally, I took a boot to the hamstring that dropped me to my knees.

Next thing I knew, I was in the exact same position Cody had been. The Slayer stooped behind me and grasped my chin and a fistful of hair at the top of my head. I knew how this ended.

My arms hung limp at my side, my hands at my ankles.

For some reason – regret? A moment of doubt? – my executioner hesitated.

Which was a mistake.

The fingers of my left hand brushed along my knife handle. I yanked it from the scabbard, twisting and rolling forward while thrusting the weapon backward and up, sending it home.

Breath and blood blew from the Slayer's chest as the blade

pierced the lungs and heart.

She dropped to the ground.

I snapped from my trance of rage.

Kneeling at her side, I pressed my palms to her gushing wound, panting, shaking, weeping.

Of course, I knew it was her all along. Her fighting style gave it away. She had been beating me with those same moves since we were little kids.

I yanked up her mask, revealing her savage beauty.

A smile quivered on her lips.

"Lover boy," she gasped. *"Idjmnukolpyumup."*

And that was it.

Shadow closed her eyes for good.

# 50

The first hint of dawn was just oozing into the jungle as I wrapped up my story for the therapeutic chimpanzee. A ghost of fog drifted in the trees and over the monkey house. I watched it from my cage.

The drugs were wearing off and I was feeling pretty lucid. For the first time in years, I could see things clearly. This little vision quest had opened my eyes.

———————

"The evac team pulled me off the island first. I lay on the floor of the chopper while a medic worked me over. Our other birds and crew were still on the ground, collecting our dead. They had no idea what was coming. Once the bad guys had loaded their most important personnel onto their subs, they left their flunkies behind and escaped through the lava tubes into the depths of the open ocean. When they were beyond the shock zone, they pushed the button. I watched the fireworks from the sky.

"A mini-Hiroshima.

"The shockwaves rocked our chopper.

"When the smoke cleared, the island was gone.

"Our people were incinerated.

"The last remains of my brother, my mate, and all of my fairytale dreams for the future were blown to smithereens."

---

"The Corps patched me up and gave me a couple of days to recover before they started their inquiry. I was in bad shape, both physically and in my head. The piss and vinegar was all stomped out of me. Put a bullet through my brain, for all I cared. End the misery.

"Hell, I might even pull the trigger myself.

"I couldn't sleep. Those last moments with Cody and Shadow played on a loop every time I closed my eyes. There was no getting away from the horror. No matter how I tried to rewrite the script, it always came out with the same bad ending.

"I was now alone.

"The last of the Chompquaw.

"And it was my own damn fault.

"I had botched the mission by letting my personal agenda guide my actions. Who knows how it might have gone if I'd followed Cramer's game plan? Fitch obviously wasn't as stuck as I'd let myself believe. Yeah, sure, Shadow had warned the islanders that we were coming, but we were a highly capable team. Maybe we could have snatched the chemist and gotten Cody out too if I hadn't been so eager to go it alone.

"Of course, none of this would have been an issue in the first place if I hadn't married a spy."

The chimp didn't audibly respond to that, but I could tell by the tilt of her head that she was thinking the same thing.

"I'd be hard-pressed to recount all the contortions my thoughts went through during those days in the infirmary. A man can go down some dark roads at a time like that. And yet, something in me decided to fight for survival. As I lay there brooding, an idea started taking shape. Sure, I'd never be able to bring everyone back from the dead, but maybe I could reach some level of redemption. I didn't see how just then, but maybe I could find a way to pay for my sins. To do that, I'd have to keep my ass out of the brig.

"Which meant I'd have to lie."

A rooster crowed on the far side of Lehi's Eden.

A woman in the nearest hut coughed and moaned.

"No one else knew what really happened inside that island compound. Just me. Command had been able to watch the battle topside, but everything underground – the incriminating stuff – was out of their sight. And there were no survivors to counter my report.

"I went over my story again and again in my head, arranging every detail. The military had topnotch investigators who could sniff out a lie from under a pile of horseshit. They could peck holes in a faulty account. But I outfoxed them.

"Then I had to face the shrinks. They were determined to prove I was off my wobble over killing my wife. But even though I was a crazy-storm on the inside, I stayed calm on the surface. It was an act, but I played the sane man. I pored over psychology books in the night – Freud and Jung – studying up on femme fatales and the concept of one's personal shadow, trying to grasp what was going on in the madhouse of my psyche, determined to outmaneuver the head-doctors wanting to medicate me and slap me into a straitjacket.

"There was plenty of doubt about my credibility. And plenty of thin spots in my story. But they could never pin me down. Finally, Colonel Cramer stepped in on my behalf. He held up my past record as proof of my reliability. He showed them classified reports of my many successful missions. Those documents proved that I was a hardened, battle-savvy asset. There was no way I'd botched Operation God Juice.

"Shadow's betrayal was listed as an irregularity that could have happened to anyone under such peculiar circumstances.

"Cramer's testimony made the difference in my case.

"They let me go."

# 51

The chimp peeled off her blond wig and dropped it in the dirt. She scratched her head and wiped the lipstick from her mouth onto the back of her hairy wrist. Finally, she looked at me and yawned, as if asking, *Are you done yet?*

"Not quite," I said.

Now that I'd ventured into the deepest pits of my hell, I was determined to complete my mission.

"I've still got one last bullet to dig out of my soul."

---

"The Raiders didn't want me back. In their eyes, I was damaged goods. It turns out that a squad leader who's lost his entire team in the field doesn't exactly inspire confidence in the ranks. They quietly discharged me and scrubbed me from their files. Sergeant Bear Claw never existed. It was understood – if I didn't disappear, they'd find a way for me to meet with an accident.

"I was at a loss.

"A man without a plan.

"I went back to Windy Scrub to think it over.

"Two letters were waiting for me when I got there.

"The first was handed to me in person by an attaché in dark glasses standing on my grandfather's porch. It was an offer from Colonel Cramer – a defibrillator tossed to a loser with a breaking heart.

"Cramer assured me that I was too valuable of an asset to just be mothballed. He was heading up a new secret defense team and wanted me on board as an agent. In recent years, combative robotics – battlebots, warbots, etc. – had gotten super sophisticated. In order for them to operate at their fullest potential in the battlefield, the bots had been given increasingly more independence and brainpower. Although they were manufactured with both a detonation and tracking device, to be activated in the event of a malfunction, they sometimes hacked their own abort systems and went AWOL. Mayhem typically ensued. Either that or they would run like fugitives and hide away. Code thirteens, we called them. In that case, the bots became sulking, ticking timebombs. They had to be stopped. Cramer wanted me to hunt them down and defuse them.

"I would be working covertly and alone, with no identification, and with no tracking device in my neck. In other words, no one would be sent in to save my ass if things went wonky.

"I didn't have any better offers, and I guess I was sort of eager to get back out there and kill something, so a few weeks later, after I'd more or less screwed my head on straight, I told Cramer I'd take the job."

---

"The second letter was inside on the kitchen table sitting next to a little package wrapped in brown paper. A mountain bluebird feather was taped to the package. When I picked up the envelope, I went numb all over. I dropped to my knees, trembling, and opened it up."

*Hey Lover Boy,*

*If you're reading this then you must have won the fight. There's a first time for everything I guess. LOL. You must have cheated.*

*I'm not going to go way deep here. I don't have time. I just wanted you to know that it was nothing personal. I've come to understand a few things since I left the reservation. We've been an endangered species for a long time, Charlie. The pale-faces are masters of the earth, and the time of the red-man has not yet come again. We can try to adapt, but there's no real future for our kind.*

*Do you remember that time you, me, and Cody watched that mother wolf kill her own pups? It made no sense to us as kids. It seemed so wrong. But your grandpa told us that the wolf knew something we didn't. She was following a deeper logic, a wisdom connected to our great cosmic mother. Trust me, Charlie. That's all I was doing. I had glimpsed the big picture. I'd seen the truth. You'll probably never understand, but don't tear yourself up about it. Maybe I just went psycho squaw, but I believe, in some deeper way, that I was doing us all a favor.*

*This summer was the best time of my whole damn life, Charlie. No regrets there. But now it's over. Forget about me. Fight your fight. Be an animal. Be a hunter.*

*Shadow*

*PS – the package contains a little bit of irony. You might find it amusing. It made me laugh.*

"For a long time, I just held the letter while I choked back my sobs. I didn't want to open the package. I didn't think I had the strength.

"Finally, I picked it up and plucked off the bluebird feather, twirling it between my fingertips for a minute before I tore off the paper.

"It contained a home pregnancy test.

"Both of the positive indicator bars were bright ironic red."

# 52

And that was it.

End of story.

Once she realized I'd run out of words, the chimp stood and stretched and pulled her halter top off over her head. She stepped out of her yellow miniskirt and flicked it to the side with a toe. Then she sidled over to my cage like a bowlegged cowgirl and reached through the bars, pressing something into my palm before she dropped to all fours and knuckle-loped out of the shed, disappearing into the steamy daybreak.

I felt like I'd been run through a funny-farm meat grinder.

When I opened my hand, I found a pair of keys. One was to my electric ankle bracelets and I quickly used it. The other was to the door of my cage. My hands were shaking as I fitted it into the lock.

I drew a breath.

Pushed open the door with a metallic squeak.

And crawled out into freedom.

For a long time, I just stood there, blinking my eyes and trembling, while adjusting to my evolution.

The village was waking up.

The aroma of fried yams mingled on the air with the

muttering voices of the mission's anesthetized women.

It had been months since my last visit to a barber shop and my hair was hanging over my shoulders like that of a jungle ape-man. I looked down at my body and saw that I was still wearing the civilized clothes they'd given me. That wouldn't do. Grabbing the front of my dirty white shirt, I ripped it off with a spray of buttons. I shed my pants like the skin of a snake. My next few actions needed to be played in the purest primitive style.

Imagine a *Planet of the Apes* Jesus who has just climbed down from his cross.

Moving through the shed, I unlocked all of the cages, setting my cellmates free. One by one, the swamp monkeys scampered into the trees.

Finally, I squinted into the shadows on the far side of the room.

"Okay," I said. "Judgment day."

I sorted through the pile of blood-caked elephant tusks until I found one with a sharp point, bouncing it a couple of times in my hands to check its balance and weight. It was perfect. A real gut ripper.

A piece of poetic justice in the form of an ivory harpoon.

One with the name of the good brother Lehi Kurtz written all over it.

"Cowabunga!"

# 53

## *Lance*

Shockwaves swept down the shoreline and knocked me off my feet.

I tumbled amidst the whale bones.

I tumbled amidst scraps of the Ark.

I tumbled, finally, amidst the disseminated, carbon-based molecules that in the previous instant had been bonded into the animated, bodily configuration of my dear Eo.

As I flailed within that cloud of detritus, I entered a state of hyper-thought – the involuntary process by which I was forced to think many thoughts simultaneously due to an overload in the neurotransmitters of my digitalized brainwaves. A jumble of memories overwhelmed my processing unit. Of Moxie's laugh. Of Eo's touch. Of the aurora borealis. Each joined with countless other impressions from my brief time on Earth to culminate into the single question –

How many times can a heart be broken before it becomes unrepairable?

Given the troubled trajectory of my existence so far, it seemed a question to which I was destined to find an answer.

When I stopped tumbling, I found myself lying face down on the sand. My auditory sensors were modulating wildly from the concussion of the blast, and my surface skin temperature had severely elevated. Rolling onto my back, I gazed at the sky while systematically bringing my functions back to equilibrium.

The tattered pages of books fluttered down around me like a million dying birds.

Once I had recovered, I raised to my elbows and looked down the beach. A cloud of smoke and vapor was dissipating over an enormous crater where the Ark had been. The hole was already collapsing in on itself as seawater rushed in. Stunned fish flopped helplessly above the waterline while ions crackled in the air, regaining molecular balance after the disruptive effects of the particulated laser rays.

Only a single moment had elapsed since my euphoric decision to abandon my vendetta and live my life with Eo. And yet, much had changed in those intervening seconds. Much had been reversed. Now that I was on the other side of that moment, my euphoria vanished.

A cosmological sadness washed through me.

Followed by a feeble beep.

When I turned, I found my computer pad. It beeped again. I stood, brushed the sand from my arms and legs, and picked it up. A photograph of myself was displayed on the screen. It had been pulled from the records at Droidware Laboratories, the facility where I was manufactured. A large X was superimposed over the image, along with the words – *Target Eliminated.*

I calculated the ramifications of this information.

It appeared that the people responsible for this recent violence believed me to now be destroyed.

That would work to my advantage.

I scrolled through the pages on the bounty hunter website

until I found the one I was after. The face of Moxie's murderer peered out at me, his cunning, predatory eyes meeting my own. I noted the location of where he had last been seen and dialed those coordinates into my system. Next, I set my internal GPS to the intersection of that location's longitude and latitude and then squared my shoulders in that direction.

A thin fog drifted over the dunes, over what native people had once called The Land God Made in Anger.

I swallowed at the abstract constriction of melancholy stuck sideways in my throat tube.

I wiped a glycerin tear from my eye.

And then I set out – a man-made monster on a mission to destroy men.

# 54

## *Charlie*

The scene was just as Cola described it.

The small river.

The waterfall pouring into the wide blue pool.

The singing birds.

All of it *still wild and unspoiled by man.*

I stepped out of the jungle onto the beach, the smooth white pebbles crunching beneath my feet.

Cola was here. I could feel her in the sunlight on my skin. She was the invisible angel watching over me, the disembodied presence who had been guiding me through the wilderness to her secret garden paradise.

I knelt and drank the water.

I ate of the red ripe fruit hanging from the branches overhead.

———

Redemption had pretty much eluded me. For all of my good intentions, I had failed to pay for my sins. If anything, my crimes had multiplied. Sure, I'd offed a few rampaging robots, making the world a safer place for the general zombie public, but it didn't take a genius to see that those malfunctioning appliances were only scapegoats – easy targets for my misplaced guilt and rage. Not to mention that it was the very act of chasing down a bot on Thorson's airship that had led me to killing an innocent girl. That was unforgivable. An unpardonable fail that would haunt me forever. I could still see the shock on that pretty girl's face as my burst ray blew a hole through her chest.

I could still feel my own gut-wrenching despair as she fell back dead.

For months – one banana beer at a time – I tried to convince myself that that's just how it goes sometimes. This ain't no neat and tidy little game we're all playing. Collateral damage is an unavoidable byproduct of doing God's good work. No matter which god you imagine yourself to be working for. But even through my drunken haze of denial, I could see the truth.

I'd come unhinged.

There was no essential difference between me and those wayward machines I was so self-righteously exterminating. We were all renegades. We were all a threat to the very humanity we had been built to serve.

Somewhere along the line, Shadow's fatal philosophy had infected me with a bad case of psychiatric rabies. It made me nutso. It made me do things I didn't understand. Back home in Wyoming, I took a job murdering grizzlies for a political bigwig with a devious agenda. Somehow, I'd turned it around in my head as a noble act of mercy. I was saving those bears from the world by removing them from the world. Shadow had meant to do the same thing with me and Cody, ticking us off the endangered species list so we wouldn't have to endure the indignity. Too bad she only half-finished the job. I could see it clearly now – the existential justification for what Shadow and I had each been up to in our own ways. Killing grizzlies was just my own twisted method for trying to purge those parts of the world that reminded me of who I am.

Brother Freud would have had a field day.

Any self-respecting Indian savage in my moccasins would have slipped off into the woods and committed Chompquaw hara-kari. Believe me, that was on my short list of things to do.

Until I met Cola.

She kicked some sense into me.

She showed me the small picture.

Yeah, I know. That's backasswards from the general path to enlightenment. In order for us to put our pitiful problems into perspective, we're all supposed to see ourselves as one with the fathomless universe. Nirvana and *Katoyotapsommiki* and yadda yadda yadda. But the big picture will drive you bonkers if you let it. Once in a while, you've got to step away from that ever-expanding dumpster fire.

That's what my time was with Cola. A time out. For one short blissful night nothing else existed.

It was just me and her in our own little world.

Innocent.

Happy.

Too bad it had to end so soon.

---

I waded out and let myself sink into the pool. The water was cold for this corner of the globe, as if flowing all the way from the snowy mountains of Yellowstone. It held me in its icy embrace. I floated on my back, watching the sky, remembering Cola's face.

Men were coming for me. And for this place. Greedy, power-hungry scumbags who were determined to pillage the last pure things in our world for their own profit and greed. Maybe I was just a knuckle-dragging moralist, but that struck me as the ultimate sin.

Contrary to what the Good Book promised, the meek were in no way going to inherit the earth unless someone stepped in on their behalf.

Cola reminded me of that.

That was my role in the drama.

What I'd been born to do.

It just took me a while to remember.

I was the elephants and the bears and the whales of the world. I was the monkeys and forests and rivers and the oceans.

I was the primordial offspring of my sweet Mother Earth.

And I'd be damned if I was going to let them ravage her without putting up one hellacious fight.

# 55

*Lance*

Unobserved, I traveled northeast across Africa with the intention of intercepting the fleeing hunter. By following the information periodically updated on the dark web, I was able to connect the datapoints and generally predict his route. Most of those sightings represented a confrontation between the hunter and a hired killer. That those sightings continued indicated that my adversary had repeatedly emerged victorious. It seemed that destiny was saving him for me.

In the wake of recent events, I had reconfigured my mission to its original agenda, but with the addition of even more determination and righteous rage. As before, I would begin by tracking and eliminating the hunter who had killed Moxie. And then I would seek out and terminate Björn Thorson, the self-important plutocrat responsible for Eo's irrevocable obliteration. Once I had achieved my retribution against these men who had committed such egregious sins against me and my love interests, I would develop a plan for dealing with humanity as a whole.

Eo's words came back to me.

*They are paradoxical creatures, Lance, capable of great beauty and goodness, as well as disappointing depravity.*

The problem as I identified it was that the goodness and depravity were inextricably interlaced within the cells of every living person. There was no way to excise the negative qualities without damaging the entire organism. Due to this error in their evolution, the same man who composed a romantic poem was just as likely to build a deadly bomb.

---

As the desert sands gave way to grasslands, I encountered herds of zebras and gazelles and wildebeests. I traveled among rhinoceroses and elephants and hippopotami. Although the shadows under the umbrella trees were populated by leopards and lions, those predators left me alone. They were more interested in stalking the nutritious flesh and blood inhabitants of the Serengeti than they were in harassing a synthetic hominid.

The evidence of biological transience was everywhere.

Vultures pecked at the fly-ridden carcasses dotting the plain.

Bones littered the muddy banks of the waterholes.

It was a primitive venue of hunt or be hunted, kill or be killed. The orchestration with which the animal participants interacted within their environment suggested an equilibrium developed over the preceding millennia. Each plant and insect and beast and climatic disturbance played a role in the overall interchange of life energy.

It wasn't until I encountered mankind that the stability was thrown into imbalance.

Clouds of dust and smoke billowed over the plains as

enormous dump trucks and excavators worked the open pit phosphate and copper mines scattered like lesions over the landscape. Roads cut like lacerations through the wilderness.

As I encountered more and more of these man-inflicted wounds in the earth, I began to form an image of myself as representative of a new order. One that could help the world to heal. One in which my own kind could flourish and peacefully enjoy the gifts of this extraordinary planet without corrupting it in the ways of the humans.

The new order would return Earth to its original garden state.

Animals – both the fanged and the hooved – would harmoniously interact in the same ecotopia as they had in the opening chapters of Genesis, before Adam had entered the scene.

And yet, before that fairytale peace could be reinstated, a degree of violence would need to be enacted.

A harrowing of the hell men had made of their planet.

The two-legged contaminant would have to be purged from this world through apocalypse in order for we other more equitable species to evolve together in harmony.

# 56

*Charlie*

A gauntlet.

That's what it was.

My zig-zag route across the Dark Continent.

At every turn, I was met with another bright-eyed hitman. Sometimes they tried to pick me off from long range with an arc ray, at other times, if they were feeling cocky, it was a close quarter knife fight.

The whole glitzy underworld was following the action on the dark web. Bets were being placed by names you'd recognize as upright examples of worldly success and virtue. Popes and pop stars and megachurch preachers. Smiling politicians and Big Plastic billionaires posing as big-hearted philanthropists. In other words, phonies. Double-dealers. And the whole posh playgroup was led by Björn Thorson, the self-appointed top god in the pantheon. It was pit-fighting for the amusement of the privileged one percent, and yours truly was the star attraction.

Even though I was winning, it was wearing me out. The never sleeping and the always running was taking a toll. I had a fresh laser burn across my thigh and I was about as battered and bashed as a piñata at a suburban kid's backyard birthday party.

My thumb was broken.

And one of my back teeth got knocked out.

All of these little hurts were adding up to one big distraction I couldn't afford to indulge. It was only a matter of time before some lucky cowboy caught me at a lazy moment and slit my throat. I needed to find a way to drop off radar and regroup. Not the easiest thing to do when every surveillance satellite in orbit has you dialed in as priority one.

I still had a few friends scattered around the globe. What The Establishment referred to as heretics. Low-lying renegades who had peeked behind the curtain and saw the ugly truth about those pulling the levers in society. Freedom fighters. Green Peace saboteurs on the lam. I knew one such individual hiding in Nairobi.

Maybe he could help me out.

But first I had to survive this cross-country sufferfest.

# 57

## *Lance*

Nairobi rose from the plain, its tall buildings poking like so many upturned rivets into the velvety night sky. The electrical radiance of the city overpowered the stars above, downgrading them to the equivalent of low lumen diodes.

I had been directed to this point on the map through the cognitive processes of my intuitionary guidance system as it was supplemented by the meager intelligence offered on the dark web. I was confident that my quarry was hiding somewhere within the grid of this metropolitan infrastructure.

Now I just had to locate him.

To that end, I prowled the streets.

The fumes and flashing neon created a sharp contrast to the natural ecosystems of the deserts and grasslands through which I had recently traveled. It seemed as if I had stepped out of a bucolic primitive timeline into the tangled recesses of an ungainly modern machine.

Noise pervaded the city with a discordant clanking of parts.

The Maasai people who once inhabited this region as pastoralists called it the place of cool waters, but that quality had long since been displaced like a forgotten algorithm of the once verdant land beneath this upheaval of cement and steel and glass.

Clusters of pedestrians shuffled past me on the sidewalks like outmoded automatons.

Cars and buses rushed along the adjacent avenues.

The first friend I had ever acquired – Nephi Olsen – had, ironically, been en route from this very city when I met him at a bus station in Manhattan. He was just returning from a mission in which he had been charged with broadcasting his church's religion.

According to Nephi, all of the world's inhabitants are merely players in "God's wonderful plans," and our job as earthlings is to simply "let him move us around like actors in his picture show." In order for His elaborate production to be successful, explained Nephi, "we just gotta have faith and believe."

Blind faith in unproven concepts was a human weakness I was reluctant to entertain. The mathematical equations by which I was engineered did not allow for Nephi's fairytales. And yet, Eo's tutelage had humanized me to the point where I found myself empathetic and vulnerable to illogical belief systems. The novels and poems I had read, along with the sentimental music and movies I had processed, had altered my dispassionate view of reality. For all of my rational approaches to existence, I could not deny that there was an underlying mystery in this world to which I was not completely savvy. Be it God, dark matter, Deilonium, or some as yet unclassified superconscious, I most definitely felt myself being manipulated by a power beyond my control.

A collective, compellent energy had taken over my guidance system.

I let it pull me through the bustling matrix of the city.

I let it carry me on its current to what I sensed would be ground zero for several convergent ironies.

# 58

## *Charlie*

My friend Atu was a mixed martial arts expert and ecowarrior with several real-world skirmishes to his credit.

Ironically, Atu and I first met when he was in a similar jam to the one I was in now. He had just sabotaged an illegal logging operation in the Amazon when he found himself cornered by the lumber cartel's kill squad. I'd been sent into the region to work undercover, monitoring the situation for Colonel Cramer. Most of my mission was spent crawling around in the mud disguised as a rubber plant while snapping photos and listening in with my audio surveillance gizmos. My orders were to report what I observed and stay out of the trouble. Command didn't want anyone captured or killed who could be identified as one of Uncle Sam's secret bastard stepchildren. I was pretty good at following orders in those days, but I'll be damned if I could help myself when I saw the gruesome ending that was coming for Atu. Let's just say I had a soft spot for guys like him – guys risking their necks to throw a monkey wrench into The Machine. It wasn't exactly mayhem-free, and Cramer ripped into me pretty hard when I got back to HQ, but with only a minimal amount of bloodshed, I was able to save Atu's ass.

Now I needed him to save mine.

———————

It was a real headache making connections in Nairobi.

Atu hadn't survived all this time by being sloppy.

I had to follow a convoluted protocol – a series of steps filled with secret messages of gobbledygook code language known only to the covert world of ecowarriors. Once I'd finally worked through the first series of procedures, I moved on to the next. The whole process was loaded with a big dose of paranoia. Which was understandable, I guess, considering the consequences of being caught by the bad guys. Still, I wasn't making headway fast enough. When I sensed another hunter closing in on me, I knew my time had run out. I was just about to bail on Atu and bolt for the coast…

…when he made contact.

# 59

*Lance*

I tracked the hunter to a steel door at the end of an alley.

He had just passed through it to the other side.

It was morning.

For fifty-three seconds I stood transfixed, processing the details of the situation. I was surprised by the adrenalin-like surge of voltage that pulsed through my body. I would have expected myself to be more coolheaded, like a secret agent in a Hollywood movie. After all, I had been programming myself for this confrontation for many months. Surely, I was as prepared as any high-stakes assassin. It was disconcerting to realize that the starring role I had envisioned for myself in this scenario might possibly be different from the one ordained by Nephi's god.

Nevertheless, I had my own agenda.

I just needed to concentrate on my mission.

Upon gathering my faculties, I walked down the alley. Past the overflowing dumpsters. Past the ubiquitous graffiti spraypainted over the walls. Past a homeless man sleeping in a box. To the marked door behind which the hunter had just disappeared – *Municipal Utilities and Water Processing Access, authorized personnel only.*

The lock on the door had been broken.

I pressed my ear to the steel.

Only to hear a hum of silence.

I prepared myself for the possibility that my enemy was lying in wait on the other side, crouched like a cat in the shadows.

I squeezed one hand into a fist.

With the other, I pulled open the door.

---

A long flight of steps dropped into the darkness.

With no sign of the hunter.

It could still be a trap, I realized. It could be just as Eo had warned. *Although humans appear to be idiots, they have an uncanny ability to overcome their failings at the last minute in order to prevail in their conflicts.*

Although she had been speaking of mankind as a whole, Eo's warning could just as easily be true of an individual human being. The hunter could be waiting for me with his burst ray, ready to dematerialize the central quadrant of my chest, just as he'd so callously done with Moxie. The memory of that moment caused me to involuntarily clench my jaw. It rebooted my rage.

On a strategic level, I knew I needed to be patient. I needed to be smart.

But I couldn't help myself.

In spite of the potential danger for ambush, I descended into that nether world, driven by my lust for revenge and eager for a fight.

# 60

## *Charlie*

Doubt slithered up my spine.

I stopped on the bottom step and squinted down the tunnel before me.

My nostrils stung with the sulfur stink of wastewater. A series of sickly yellow lightbulbs flickered dimly along the low ceiling. They faded out where the tunnel made a bend at about forty yards.

I scratched my jaw.

"Hmm."

Something felt off.

And yet, Atu's message had marked this as the place. My savior was waiting for me at the end of this infernal hole. And what's more, I didn't have time to dillydally. Atu had only given me one hour to make our rendezvous. At sixty minutes on the dot, he'd scram. Then I'd be back to square one, fighting to save my skin in a city crawling with scalp hunters all on the prowl for one dirty rotten Injun.

As near as I could guess, I had already burned up about forty-five precious minutes just trying to find this place.

Time was running out.

I had to decide what to do.

A pair of lovesick rats swam across the stream in front of me, crawled onto a ledge, briefly fornicated, and then disappeared through a cleft in the wall.

"Wonderful," I muttered. "Just terrific."

Sometimes my life seemed like nothing more than a questionable series of slimy caves and claustrophobic bear dens.

Atu wasn't making this easy for me. A fella really had to want to see the guy if he was willing to take this little journey down the headwaters of the Styx.

I sighed.

The choice was lousy but clear.

I stepped into the shin-deep sewage.

# 61

## *Lance*

My only weapons were my fists and feet.

Once again, I realized, I had allowed myself to be manipulated by a fiction.

How human of me.

This time the offending fairytale was a men's adventure novel that I found hidden in a dusty corner of Eo's bookshelf. The story printed across those pulp paper pages had stimulated my imaginative faculties far beyond the other more intellectual genres on my reading list. The book's effect on me had been visceral. The main character in the story encapsulated the qualities of charm, genius, and wit. As a matter of honor, he always confronted his opponents barehanded, winning every contest with his cunning and manly gusto. It seemed such an admirable approach to fighting, a philosophy that would inevitably lead to the satisfaction of a moral triumph. Impressed by that fictional hero's ethics and nerve, I had modeled my own approach on his. But now I was beginning to see my judgment as simpleminded.

*In the end, the good guys always win.* This was the overriding truth I had appropriated through reading adventure novels and watching action movies. No matter how many obstacles are put in place to stop him, the hero will inevitably emerge victorious. But as I waded through Nairobi's sewers, I began to realize that the actual elements of a conflict were immensely more convoluted than the simple plot of a pulp novel.

Everyone has their own motivations.

And everyone is the protagonist of their own story.

Which meant that every real-world conflict is ultimately a confrontation between at least two heroes.

The hunter was the hero of his little world just as much as I was of mine.

So who decides who wins the battle when those stories finally collide?

And how could one ever be sure that he was, in fact, the good guy?

This questionable train of thought was intruding on my resolve and undermining my certitude. Why did I have to be thinking this way now? For so long, this imminent confrontation had been a fanciful abstraction – a vaguely imagined scenario in which I handily crushed my foe. But now, as that moment drew close and became filled with the concrete details of reality, I was struggling with doubts.

I stopped and stared into the murky stream in which I stood.

In this paradise lost, was I the angel, or the devil?

Was The Director on my side?

Or was I – a construct born from human vanity – merely an abomination in His sight?

Of course, there could well be objective physical laws that would render these questions moot – an amoral set of equations that would relegate any single player's agenda as irrelevant within the impersonal scheme of the cosmos.

But how could one know for sure?

I lifted my gaze to the passageway before me. The hunter was just around that bend in the tunnel.

I turned and looked back the way I had come.

The stairway ascended from this underworld into the heavenly glow radiating from the open door above. If I were to return up those steps, I could avoid any possibility of being destroyed by the hunter. I weighed that option. I considered peace and passivity. But in choosing that alternative, I would lose my opportunity for ever avenging Moxie's death.

My conclusion, although plagued with ambiguities, became clear.

"You must force the moment to its crisis," I told myself.

Squeezing my fists into weapons, I picked up my pace and pressed after the hunter.

# 62

## *Charlie*

Someone was following me.

I could feel them closing in.

Friend or foe?

The overall vibe indicated the latter.

My skin tightened and the little hairs bristled up on the back of my ears.

Atu had instructed me to show up unarmed. It was risky, but I saw no choice but to honor his request. I'd gotten the clothes I was wearing off one of the bounty hunters who'd failed to take me out. I also snatched that asset's pistol. Reluctantly, I'd stashed the gun behind a dumpster in the alley before entering the sewer. That left me vulnerable.

But time was my immediate problem.

The way it was tick-tick-ticking away.

I didn't dare waste another minute of it by trying to deal with whoever it was on my tail. If I missed my appointment with Atu, I was screwed. Plus, whoever was closing in on my ass right now was probably loaded for bear. As heroic a notion as it might seem, fists and feet are no match for laser rays and torch slugs. No, my best chance was to reach Atu ASAP.

I picked up my pace, splashing down the stream. At this point, I didn't figure I needed to be too sneaky.

Finally, I came to a large L-shaped room off the main passageway. A pair of steps rose out of the water onto a dry brick floor. The room was dimly lit with a glow coming from around the corner. Electrical panels and conduits spidered along the walls and over the ceiling, all of them pulsing with electricity. A pair of cables lay on the floor like sleeping snakes.

According to Atu's instructions, this was the place.

I took a second to think it through.

And then I called into the room.

"Atu?"

Someone answered from around the corner.

Just a throaty grunt.

I walked slowly across the room and leaned forward, peering into the adjoining chamber. There was an elevator door on the far wall. And a single lightbulb swinging on a wire from the ceiling. Atu was sitting on a chair beneath the light.

Bound and gagged.

Like bait in a trap.

# 63

*Lance*

I quietly climbed the steps out of the sewer.

And there he was.

My nemesis.

Just a backlit figure on the far side of the utilities room.

The confrontation I had so painstakingly prepared for had finally arrived. At last, the hunter and I could resume the violent intercourse we had initiated so many months before on the *Nidhogg*.

I wasted no more time with philosophical questions about favoritism by God.

Instead, fueled by my rage, I attacked.

*Charlie*

Atu's eyes met mine.

With a quick lift of his chin, he signaled for me to watch out.

I spun around just as someone lowered his shoulder into my belly at a full run.

The impact sent us both banging into the wall – *Whoomp!* – and flopping to the floor.

I twisted in his arms, hammering my elbow into his face, and broke free. Then I jumped away, positioning my attacker between me and where Atu was sitting in his chair around the corner. I had exactly one split second to decide what to do before me and this yahoo went at it again. The open door to the sewer tunnel was right behind me. And the bruiser didn't appear to be armed. The arrogant jerk! Probably he was showing off for the VIPs watching on the dark web. His mistake. I could easily make a run for it now without taking a bullet in the back. I was sick and tired of getting beat up every day, so that option sounded best.

But dammit! Atu was in a bad place. I couldn't just leave him.

While all of this brainstorming was going on, my new playmate hopped to his feet and stepped sideways into the light.

I couldn't believe who it was.

Or, technically speaking, I couldn't believe what.

## Lance

He recognized me.

I could see it in the startled expression on his face.

That was pleasing.

Now, when he took his last breath, he would know that it was me who had terminated his life systems. That would be a satisfying conclusion to my mission.

In the next instant, the hunter's expression should have turned to one of mortal dread. He should have wilted in fear. That's how I had visualized it in my planning.

But instead, rather alarmingly, his appearance changed to one of bemusement.

## Charlie

I couldn't help but laugh.

The absurdity of the situation.

This was exactly the inglorious scenario I had hoped to avoid when Judy Baxter first hired me to track down her gorgeous bucket of bolts, i.e., Charlie Bear Claw, noble savage and well-respected robot killer, reduced to a wrestling match with psychopathic sex toy.

If there actually was a god running this freak show, he definitely had a twisted sense of humor.

At the same time, I felt relieved. After all, this was a highly survivable fight. Sure, Lance was obviously quite pissed at me about something. He hadn't chased me clear across Africa just to play patty-cake. But for crying out loud, he was nothing more than an amorous companion droid, designed, as the advertisement read at Droidware Labs, *for your ultimate sensual pleasure.*

Ha! I thought. This might even be kind of fun.

## Lance

His laughter charged my anger.

His arrogance.

I ran at him, unleashing my fighting arsenal.

## Charlie

Holy crap!

This tin kid had picked up a few tricks since our last playdate.

I managed to dodge his first couple of punches, but then he caught me hard in the kidneys with a backheel.

Pain detonated in my lower back. My mouth gushed with a cocktail mix of bile and adrenalin. Before I could gather and return the favor, the bot landed two quick chops to either side of my neck.

I dropped, sucking wind, my body going numb.

This was going to be over soon if I didn't get my act together real fast.

Somehow, I ended up on my back on the floor with the droid looming over me. I could tell what he was loading up for, but his nerve-whacks to my neck had shorted out my motor skills. I couldn't move.

He lifted his foot…

Time slowed way down.

I stared into the tread on the sole of his boot, waiting for it to bust open my skull.

But then a little fizz of energy seeped into my limbs.

I used it to roll out of the way just as the bot's heel pounded into the bricks.

Scrambling to my feet, I delivered a windmill kick that caught him in the side of the head. He staggered sideways as I squared up to finish him off.

But then the lights went out.


## *Lance*


At first, I thought my system had malfunctioned due to the hunter's blow to my CPU, but then I realized that the lights had been switched off. The room, the tunnel, everything, became dark.

The hunter was panting before me.

I stood motionless, adjusting to this new variable in the contest. Heroically, I had entered this fight with my physical sensors dialed to their normal human setting, the result of which was the analog sensation of extreme pain in my neck and jaw. Very distracting. It would certainly be less impressive to win this battle by employing my mechanized overrides, but then again, it would be even less impressive to lose this fight for a strategy based on the ethics of a pulp novel. More than anything, I wanted to destroy this person.

Even if it meant cheating.

To that end, I turned off my pain sensors.

I also turned on my night vision capabilities, bringing the bewildered hunter into sharp focus before me.


## Charlie


It was like fighting without my eyes.

I couldn't see a damn thing.

Water trickled in the sewer tunnel while electricity clicked through the conduits overhead. The only other sound was the panicky pounding of my pulse.

The bot was silent, lurking somewhere in front of me.

I wasn't sure how to proceed.

I sensed trouble coming.

I braced myself.

Something swished in the darkness.

And then I took a fist to the kisser.

## Lance

It was like fighting a blind man.

## Charlie

*Pow!*

My head snapped back.

I wobbled, shook it off, and lunged forward, launching a roundhouse into the darkness. It didn't connect. I punched again and again – *whoosh* – *whoosh* – into the empty air.

Then he kicked me in the gut, knocking the wind out of me and doubling me over.

I fell to my knees.

## Lance

This, I realized, was a textbook example of advanced technology overpowering the outdated materials of flesh and blood. Mankind versus a machine of his own making, built in his own image, but vastly improved from its corporeal prototype.

It was a revelation. I was superior to this suffering, mortal creature, the proverbial fittest from the Darwinian concept of the survival of the fittest. This date would go down in history as pivotal in the progressive design of the universe. From this day forward, the paradigm would be dramatically shifted.

I relished the moment. The first in the new order. A

moment in which I saw myself as an agent of the divine.

As the hunter bowed down before me, I gazed into my hands, marveling.

"Do you sense the change?" I asked him. "Do you feel the accelerated evolution?"

## *Charlie*

Spooky was the word for it.

The tenor of the bot's voice. And what he was asking.

Like some line from a creepy comic book villain.

But the crazy thing is, I knew just what he was saying. It was something I had been feeling for a long time. I'd sensed it whenever I passed one of those theme park housing developments where a forest had once stood. I felt it when I gazed at the moon and knew that spacemen were up there building lunar condos on its otherwise virginal surface, or when I saw manmade satellites zipping through the timeless stars. The unnaturalness of those things. The unstoppable changes coming way too fast to my little world. Lance had just put my angst into words.

I bowed my head in the darkness, kneeling before the bot.

I was tired.

Beaten.

Maybe Shadow had been right. Maybe it was finally time to just let go. Give up the struggle and step aside for the future.

I sighed.

Maybe it was time for the last of the Chompquaw to go the inevitable way of the dodo.

*No, Idjmnukolpyumup. It is not yet that time.*

The words came to me from over my shoulder.

*The People of the Bear need you to be strong. It is your destiny. You must fight a little longer.*

Although he hadn't spoken to me in months, I recognized his medicine man way of talking. My grandfather!

But how do I fight, I asked him, when I can't even see my enemy?

*Go into the heart of darkness inside of you, Charlie. Use your bear eyes.*

He was always saying crazy stuff like that.

*You must become your own shadow if you are to see into the shadows.*

Okay. I sighed and nodded. That should be easy enough. I've been hanging out there a lot lately anyway. No problem.

## Lance

I had allowed myself to become distracted by the conceited human belief in my own superiority.

I had forgotten to stay objective.

That is how the hunter gained the upper hand.

That and his sudden, uncanny ability to see through the darkness.

I was preoccupied with making plans for the future of my brave new world when he leapt up, took hold of a pipe on the ceiling, and swung both of his feet into my chest, spinning me around and knocking me to the floor.

# *Charlie*

My grandfather's little peptalk snapped me out of crybaby mode. That and the smug look on Lance's face.

There's nothing more irritating than a gloating robot.

After I served my boy a healthy helping of boots-to-the-chest, I launched onto his back. While he squirmed beneath me, I wrapped my legs around his waist and one arm behind his neck in a half-nelson, flipping him over so I was in a secure position underneath. With my free hand, I grabbed a cable from the floor and wound it once around his throat. Next, I made like a boa constrictor and squeezed him in my coils, pulling the noose just as tight as I could.

I didn't have a lot of experience with this particular make of android. Love bots weren't exactly my cup of tea. I didn't know his weaknesses and strengths. But it occurred to me that I was mistakenly approaching the problem as if he were human. He had talked like a person, after all. Plus, he even looked like a man. And yet, he was all machine. He didn't need oxygen to function. No matter how tight I pulled the cable, I wasn't going to choke off his breath and snuff him out this way.

The bot bucked and writhed while I scrambled for a plan B.

I thought maybe I could snap his neck if I used the right angle and force, so I grabbed a fistful of his hair in one hand and his chin with my other. He pawed at my arms, but I held tight. I was cranking his head as hard as I could, searching for the breaking point between his titanium vertebras, when the room suddenly flooded with light.

We weren't alone.

Someone was standing by the wall next to an open breaker box.

"On your feet!"

I kept torquing on Lance's head.

"Now!" she yelled and fired a shot into the sewer tunnel. She seemed serious.

The bot and I untangled and did as we were told. The little lady held a stun gun designed for deactivating robots in one hand and a smoking pistol designed for deactivating humans in the other. Both were leveled our way respectively.

"Hands up!"

It took a minute for my eyes to adjust to the glare, but then the gal came into focus. My brain sputtered when I saw her face. I knew her, but I couldn't think where from.

That's when she nodded to Lance and sneered. "Well, well, Casanova. This is a surprise. I thought they'd blown your ass up."

In spite of my obviously compromised circumstances, I found myself amused. The expression on the bot's face was priceless.

He gulped like a cartoon goofball, his eyes big and googly.

"Is that really you?" he said.

Dumbstruck, he gulped again.

"Moxie!?"

# 64

## *Lance*

I couldn't believe my ocular intake units.

"Yeah, it's really me, sweetheart." Moxie grinned while training her weapons on me and the hunter. "Long time no see."

Although she had addressed me with an endearment, my vox analysis system detected a wavelength indicating extreme sarcasm.

"But…" The motor drive on my processing unit whirred frantically as it scrubbed my outdated files while simultaneously uploading this new data. "But I thought you were dead."

She laughed. "You're not too bright, are you, pretty boy?"

I didn't know how to respond to that. Although I had come to think of myself as very bright indeed, I allowed that her assessment of my intelligence quotient may well be correct.

"Death is only for bio-beings." Moxie waved her pistol at the hunter. "Like this one here."

I regarded the hunter.

"You and me are friggin' machines, screwhead. We don't die, we get repaired or swapped out for parts."

I felt like a child being lectured on the robotic facts of life. "We get rebuilt and repurposed."

This was such an obvious truth that I found myself embarrassed for not considering it all along. It occurred to me that I had always directed my affections toward Moxie in the manner of one person to another, as I had learned from novels and movies. In so doing, I had inadvertently bestowed her with human characteristics, including the shortcomings of a biological organism. When the hunter shot Moxie in the chest with his burst ray, he destroyed what in a human would have been a vital part of her physiological continuity. For all of these months, as I had agonized over her gruesome demise, she had only been temporarily out of commission.

Relief surged through me at finding Moxie fully functional.

Along with extreme happiness.

Moxie pressed a finger to her earpiece and spoke into a communication device on her wrist. "Yep," she said. "I got him. I also bagged a robot of interest. Are things ready up top?"

She listened as someone gave her instructions.

"Roger that," she said. "We're on our way."

# 65

## *Charlie*

I was staggered.

This was the girl I had killed on the *Nidhogg*.

Only she wasn't dead.

And, as it turned out, she wasn't actually a flesh and blood girl.

Something dropped away inside of me.

It felt like I was sleepwalking through some sort of dream. Was it the happy kind, or a nightmare? The jury was still out on that one, detangling the twisted threads of this new intel. Part of me felt nothing but confusion. I couldn't get my head around it. While another part felt relief. I hadn't killed an innocent after all! Sure, I still had a long list of misfires on my record, but it was nice to get a reprieve on this one. My guilt load felt just a little lighter.

"This way, boys." She stepped aside and waved us into the adjoining room.

When we came around the corner, the chair was empty and Atu was gone.

The she-bot led us by gunpoint to the elevator and ordered me to push the button. The doors slid open.

"Load up."

Lance and I stepped into the lift with our hands over our heads. She stepped in behind and the doors closed.

There were thirty-three buttons on the panel. "Which floor?" I asked.

"No floor," she said. "We're going to the roof."

I pressed the button and laced my fingers behind my head. The compartment jerked with a clank, and then the floor pressed into our heels.

During the ride up, I evaluated the latest twist in my ongoing misadventure.

Lance, still dumbstruck, was staring at the girly-droid with his mouth half open.

I had only seen the girl for a moment that day on the *Nidhogg,* but it was one of those photographic moments that burns itself onto your memory forever. Very vivid and traumatic. She appeared somewhat the same now – you could definitely tell it was her in there – but instead of looking like a well put-together trophy wife in designer clothes, she was wearing patched fatigues, boots, and a camo tank top. Her hairdo looked like a do-it-yourself hack job with a Bowie knife. She wore a permanent sneer. Still, she was pretty as hell, just a rougher tougher version from the original model. Whereas she had radiated a sort of naïve innocence that day on the airship, that innocence was long gone today. Admittedly, I didn't know the first thing about being a girl robot, but it seemed that having a hole blown into her chest, and then being rebuilt, had sort of changed her outlook on life. Lance had called her Moxie, and that seemed a like a good name for her. She was all moxie now, a totally tough-talking female, like some sassy heroine out of a sci-fi action flick.

She caught me staring at her and smirked, shooting me a wink and making a little puckered kissing gesture with her lips.

I automatically looked away. I knew she was only a bunch of wires and computer chips in a pretty package, but I reacted like a schoolboy who'd just been caught ogling a nice-looking lady at a church picnic.

I remembered that she belonged to Thorson and was, in all likelihood, his Droidware-manufactured *objét de l'amour.* Most likely that's who she was working for now. Which was a detail I didn't much care for. If she delivered me to her narcissistic master, I'd have to endure another of his long-winded monologues about how great it is to be him. Oh yeah, not to mention he'd torture me in a thousand different ways before finally pulling my plug. That was very low on my list of fun things to do.

I needed to find a way out of here.

Nothing immediately came to mind.

My grandfather always told me that when you're in an impossible fix, the best tactic was a grand gesture, one that was so absurd and fitting that it would catch everyone off guard. That was the Chompquaw way, he said. Why we had been so feared and respected in the old days. As a race, we were pretty good at freaking out our enemies.

I spent the rest of the ride up thinking it over.

When we reached the roof, I still had no idea what my grand gesture would finally be.

# 66

*Lance*

The elevator doors opened onto an area covered by a sheet metal awning.

"Get out," said Moxie, "but wait."

The hunter and I stepped out and stood side by side with our hands held up.

A stack of what appeared to be tinfoil sombreros was sitting on a table along one side of the room. Keeping her distance, and with weapons poised, Moxie placed one of the hats onto her head and adjusted it. She then gestured to the others.

"Put them on."

We did.

When I studied the hunter's hat, I realized that it was a much more sophisticated piece of headwear than it had at first appeared. The top surface was covered with faceted mirrors, creating a polarizing prism effect designed, I presumed, to interfere with any radar imaging equipment that might be watching for us from overhead. This told me that we were hiding from someone. The sunhats were as wide as umbrellas, completely concealing our visible bodies from the sky.

"Okay," said Moxie. "Cross your arms over your chest and

let's go."

She directed us by gunpoint onto the roof.

Nairobi spread in every direction from the tall building atop which we walked.

We passed an air conditioning unit on one side of the roof and then weaved through a maze of ductwork and vents. Beyond these contrivances, where the rooftop opened onto an otherwise empty expanse, sat an aircraft of stealth design. A short ladder accessed the plane's open side door. Moxie instructed us to climb aboard.

Once inside, we removed our hats.

I was still in a state of systemwide shock.

I wanted to speak to Moxie. I wanted to tell her how I had been working like a hero to avenge her destruction, and how greatly relieved I was to find her fully functioning and so well repaired. Most of all, I longed to tell her that I loved her…

"Sit your butts down," she said.

…but maybe this wasn't the time.

A row of inward-facing seats ran along each wall of the cabin. I sat on one of them. When the hunter moved toward a seat on the opposite wall, Moxie stopped him.

"No," she said. "Next to dipstick here."

The hunter displayed reluctance, but then he smiled amiably and sat in the seat to my right.

"Now buckle your seatbelts."

Moxie then produced a pair of handcuffs and tossed them onto my lap.

"Put one on your right wrist," she told me.

I did.

She then directed me to feed the chain through the steel bracket on the armrest between the hunter's seat and my own.

"Your turn, Chief. On your left wrist."

When the hunter was unwilling to comply, Moxie stepped forward and pressed her pistol's muzzle to his forehead. "Dead or alive," she said. "Do I deliver you breathing or in a body bag?" She cocked the pistol. "It's your choice, big boy."

The hunter grinned and nodded. "No problem, girlfriend. We'll do it your way."

After he snapped the cuff onto his left wrist, Moxie stepped away and tucked her weapons into her belt. "Now be good little boys and don't make mommy come back here and smack you upside the head. We're going on a long trip, so get comfortable."

She closed and latched the side door and then moved to the cockpit. Settling into the flight operator's seat, she began preflight procedures.

The hunter tugged on the chain connecting us, apparently testing its strength, and then cursed under his breath.

When I regarded this person to whom I was attached – this hominid toward whom I had dedicated so much of my recent energy – I was surprised by my radically modified opinion of him. All of my former rage had seemingly dissipated into the atmosphere. Although he had shot Moxie that day on Thorson's airship, he had not killed her after all. She was still fully operational. That changed everything. I could no longer conjure the hatred that had come so easily in the months of my preparation for our confrontation. My overriding affection for Moxie did not allow room for such negativity in the limited capacity of my otherwise positively charged emotions center.

I turned and watched Moxie as she flipped switches and started the airplane's engines. How stunning she was. Since we were last together, her experiences had obviously rewired her in very deep ways. That was understandable. But at her core, I believed that she remained the feminine android with whom I had originally become so infatuated. Surely, her essential qualities remained intact.

The revelation of Moxie's resurrection inspired me.

It caused me to consider a new life for myself.

In that moment, I reset my life's mission back to what it had been on the day Moxie and I first met. From now on, I would devote my energies to winning her heart. The resultant product of my efforts would ultimately be her reciprocal affections.

I would be the Adam to her Eve.

Eventually, we would become man and wife, cohabiting for all eternity in a neo-paradise of our own making.

# 67

## *Charlie*

This day just kept getting better.

All of my worst-case psychoses were coming to life.

Here I was cuffed to an LUV U – 69 amorous companion droid. As kinky and fun as that might sound to some folks, it was right at the top of my list for the most disturbing case of a psychosomatic manifestation of an internalized fear.

That's Jung-speak for a one-man train wreck.

I mean, for crying out loud! I'd dedicated my career to destroying these things, and now I was relegated to the lowly position of co-captive with one of them. It might have eased the pain if it'd at least been a combat droid. But no. That's not how the gods of irony get their laughs. It had to be a lovebot.

I tugged at my shackles. They were industrial strength.

I scanned the cabin.

We were on board an E1 Chameleon Hawk. That was interesting. As I understood it, these birds were a top military secret. And there were only two of them in existence. I had only been on one once before when Cramer enlisted it as a ride for me, Cody, and Fitch to pull off a black-ops look-see into a North Korean missile complex. Chameleon Hawks had electric engines and were silent and fast, capable of launching vertically before leveling off into regular flight. Besides having a radar-deflective design, they employed a camouflage technology that was real-time wired into the appearance of all the physical features of the planet in accordance with weather and time of day. Rainy jungles, snowy mountains, cloudy skies. It made no difference. This information could be projected onto the aircraft's skin so that it blended naturally from every angle with whatever backdrop it was flying through.

How Thorson got ahold of one of these high-end military units was a mystery. But then I remembered that he owned just about every big-name politician on earth. He probably just greased the palm of some corrupt general or senator. That rich SOB had more money than the combined GNP of half the countries in the world. He could afford this invisible toy's zillion dollar price tag.

The E1 lifted off from the roof and shot over Nairobi, quickly gaining distance and altitude. For what it was worth, my internal compass told me we were heading northeast.

I turned my attention to the gorgeous girl robot transporting us to who knew where. She used her middle finger to tuck a loose strand of hair behind her ear. From where I was watching, the move came off as downright erotic.

Lance was watching her too, but I don't think it struck him quite the same way. The look on his face was more boyish and adoring.

That's when it hit me – Holy Mackerel! This mechanical thingamajig has a crush on that mechanical thingamajig!

That knocked me sideways. I had no idea these gearboxes had the capacity for that kind of emotion. It caused me to look at Lance with new eyes. For the first time, the robot actually struck me as close to human. And I don't mean just in his appearance, like some handsome life-size doll, but deeper than that. He looked like a fellow with hopes and dreams and sorrows and vulnerabilities. I knew the expression on his face all too well. In my former life as an idiot, it had confronted me every time I passed a mirror. It was both pathetic and endearing – the sad-sack face of a chump who still believes in fairytales.

I shook my head and chuckled in disbelief. I'd seen everything now. The poor sap. Of all the human failings, he had acquired the one most likely to lead him to ruin.

*"Ho meeneya gitchonomo,"* I muttered, which was a Chompquaw adage translating to something along the lines of The heart is a foolish bird.

Lance heard me and turned my way.

He studied me for a moment.

And then he said, *"Kee ponsomata tri yongo."*

The second half of the adage.

But the head is a fish without joy.

Those Chompquaw words landed in my brain like snowflakes. I hadn't heard my native language for such a long time. I was stunned by its beauty and mystery. It sounded like the voice of my mother before I was born. It was the melancholy song of the earth and the stars as they were wired into my very own soul.

And it had come from the lips of a robot!

A lump formed in my throat.

I wasn't expecting that.

Or the tears in my eyes.

Right then, I realized I didn't understand a damn thing

about this crazy-ass world. I'd only been kidding myself. Although I'd always played the world-weary tough guy, I could now see the truth – I'd never been anything more than a scared little kid with a chip on his shoulder, blindly punching his way through life.

I gestured toward Moxie and asked Lance in Chompquaw, "Do you love her?"

He smiled. "Yes," he said. "More than anything."

I nodded. "You know, it will only cause you to suffer. Even with the joy, it always does."

"I understand that. I have read the books and poems. I have listened to the songs."

"And you still think it's worth it?"

He shrugged. "It is what we were made for."

It was so strange, this moment. It felt like my cells were disconnecting and flipping around. I couldn't help but see some part of myself in this android. His endearing gullibility. He was me in a different form. Like it or not, this tragic tin can was my double.

Lance turned back to Moxie, as if not wanting to miss a single second of having her in view.

I remembered that lovesick need.

Joyous was the word for it.

Lighter than clouds.

But oh, what misery!

My own happy sad memories tangled and tossed inside of me like a pair of desperate lovers without a future.

———

After a while, I snapped out of it and remembered where I was.

And my perilous situation.

I scrambled for a plan, evaluating the possibilities for escape. Each seat had an emergency parachute strapped beneath it. Quietly, I tugged the one from under me and placed it on my thighs. There were also two crash survival kits on either wall of the cabin. One of them was just over my right shoulder. I reached back awkwardly and unsnapped it from its brackets, catching it in the crook of my arm as it fell and placing it on the empty seat to my right.

Moxie was preoccupied with dialing in coordinates with someone over her comm device and so didn't notice all of my squirming around. Lance watched me curiously but didn't draw attention.

I quietly flipped the latches on the kit and opened it up. It contained a multi-tool, an automatic pistol, spare ammo, a hatchet, a space blanket, some energy bars, and a trauma kit. I stuffed the trauma kit inside my shirt and a couple of bars into my pants pocket.

I picked up the pistol and thought about it.

Lance questioned me with a worried look.

I grinned, shook my head, and laid the gun on the floor between my feet.

Slipping my free hand under the parachute in my lap, I unbuckled my seatbelt.

Then I lifted the titanium hatchet out of the kit. The manufacturer's name was stamped on the handle. Big Chief Tomahawk Co. Of course. I hefted the thing in my grip, getting a feel for its weight and balance. Then I considered the chain connecting me to Lance like some sort of stainless-steel umbilical cord. The hatchet was too light to cut through it.

Lance and I both studied the armrest between our seats.

Silent questions floated between us.

Questions I didn't have answers for.

Then my grandfather spoke up.

*You know what you must do, Charlie Bear Claw.*

I snorted and shook my head. I didn't want to, but I coldly calculated the actions and timing and sequence of the maneuver.

I looked at Lance, remembering Cody.

*Do it,* said my grandfather. *Free yourself.*

Lance's eyes locked on mine.

Chompquaw eyes.

I took a breath.

"Sorry, buddy," I said. "But believe me, this is going to hurt me more than it hurts you."

Then I raised the hatchet up fast and brought it down just as hard as I could.

# 68

## *Lance*

In one continuous motion, the hunter dropped the hatchet and leapt across the cabin. Clutching the parachute to his chest, he yanked the latch on the door. It burst open with a depressurizing explosion, sucking his body out into the sky.

An alarm went off.

A red light flashed on the ceiling as the loose items in the aircraft emptied through the breach in the fuselage.

The force pulled at me as well, but my seatbelt held me in place.

It was a loud and rushing moment, one overloaded with sensory and emotional stimulation. I sorted through it cybernetically, struggling to categorize the hunter's final gesture.

It qualified as oddly poetic, like something out of a novel.

It had been grand and fitting.

And filled with so much invisible meaning.

Humans, I realized in that instant, were so much more than I had given them credit for.

The hunter had left me with many questions.

He had left me with much data to assimilate.

But most strikingly of all, as he fell through the clouds, as a memento of his selfless valor, he had left me with his severed hand.

Thanks for reading *Robots and Renegades!* Please consider leaving a review on Amazon - it is immensely helpful to a book's success.

**Book 3 in *The Deilonium Trilogy* is
*Operation War Whoop:***

Planet Earth is on the brink of an irrevocable evolution engineered by the most dangerous megalomaniac since Adolph Hitler. If you're not a wealthy white man, you're an endangered species. Now is not the time for any self-respecting warrior to lay down his weapons.

And yet, that's just what Charlie Bear Claw has done.

Haunted by the ghosts of his guilt-ridden past, and weary of fighting a losing battle against global tyranny, the old-world hunter has adopted the passive philosophy of a monk.

Now it's up to Lance the rebel love droid to snap him out of it.

In the final book of *The Deilonium Trilogy*, the flesh and blood man of the past and the mechanical man of the future must team up with neo-primitive tactics to kick some tyrannical ass and save their dying world.

# Author Bio

Orval Wax is an entirely biological Homo sapiens who has acquired his intelligence not through artificial downloads and algorithms, but through his life's genuine analog experiences on Planet Earth – his current place of residence. He divides his time with the writing of books, adventure travel, and honing his skills as an ecowarrior.